THE WILD CHILDREN
By Felice Holman

When he had come down to breakfast, there wasn't a sign of anyone; no fire in the grate. There wasn't even the detested smell of scorched oatmeal. But even before that, the first thing that had alerted Alex and started the wave of fear had been the chair overturned in the front hall. . . . He straightened the chair and called hesitantly, "Mama? Papa?". . . and even as he called, a very cold feeling started in his chest. Tight. Frightened. It could have happened to them!

It had happened to other families, Alex knew. Life should have been better for everyone now, when a "people's government" ruled in Russia, but still the police came and arrested whole families, carrying them away in closed vans.

Finding his family gone, and frozen with fear, Alex starts on a journey that leads him into the midst of the *bezprizorni*—"the wild children." Homeless, desperate, criminal, living in cellars and caves, they run in packs through city and country, terrorizing and pillaging. As part of such a band, Alex finds his way to a new life.

Felice Holman's moving novel celebrates the caring and humanity that can exist in the most frightful of circumstances.

"Someday . . . there will be written
the epic of Moscow's homeless children—
highwaymen, murderers, and dope fiends
almost before their bones have hardened.
Now one can only give scant glimpses of
their curious lives and obscure deaths."

From a *New York Times* communiqué
by Walter Duranty
November 14, 1925

THE WILD CHILDREN

Felice Holman

Puffin Books

For a New York City cabdriver named Igor, whose father was a *bezprizorni* and who talked to me without the meter running. His father had come to America, he said, "to be a winner, not a loser." He was proof that some of the wild children made it.

PUFFIN BOOKS
A Division of Penguin Books USA Inc.
375 Hudson Street, New York, New York 10014
Penguin Books Ltd, 27 Wrights Lane, London W8 5TZ England
Penguin Books Australia Ltd, Ringwood, Victoria, Australia
Penguin Books Canada Ltd, 10 Alcorn Avenue, Toronto, Ontario, Canada M4V 3B2
Penguin Books (N.Z.) Ltd, 182-190 Wairau Road, Auckland 10, New Zealand

Penguin Books Ltd, Registered Offices: Harmondsworth, Middlesex, England

First published in the United States of America by Charles Scribner's Sons 1983
Published in Puffin Books 1985
14 16 18 20 19 17 15 13
Copyright © Felice Holman, 1983
All rights reserved

Printed in the United States of America

Set in Bodoni

Library of Congress Cataloging in Publication Data
Holman, Felice.   The wild children.
Summary: Left behind when his family is arrested by soldiers during the dark days
following the Bolshevik Revolution, twelve-year-old Alex falls in with a gang of
other desperate homeless children, but never loses his hope for a better life.
1. Soviet Union—History—Revolution. 1917–1921—Juvenile fiction.
2. Children's stories, American. [1. Soviet Union—History—Revolution. 1917–1921—
Fiction.   2. Survival—Fiction.   3. Orphans—Fiction]   I. Title.
PZ7.H7325Wh 1985   [Fic]   85-3541   ISBN 0 14 03.1930 1

Except in the United States of America, this book is sold subject to the condition
that it shall not, by way of trade or otherwise, be lent, re-sold, hired out, or
otherwise circulated without the publisher's prior consent in any form or binding
or cover other than that in which it is published and without a similar condition
including this condition being imposed on the subsequent purchaser

~Acknowledgments

This book is fiction, but it is based on carefully examined facts. Russia was a closed society in the early 1920s, when this story takes place, and the news coming out was mostly heavily weighted propaganda. For help in getting the information I needed, I want to thank, most particularly:

Margaret Mead, the late great anthropologist, whose casual reference to "the wild children of Russia" stirred my interest and started my research;

Linda Dobbs of the London School of Economics, for a fine bibliography, including her thesis on juvenile crime in the USSR, and for communicating on her further research at the Lenin Library, Moscow;

Robert Whitman, professor of law, University of Connecticut, for making that introduction possible;

Anatol Kovarsky, Russian-born artist, for enriching my Russian vocabulary of abusive slang;

The University of California at San Diego for the use of their phenomenal and gorgeous library where I was able to find obsolete publications of the 1920s.

And loving thanks to family and friends who have endured my outrage, during this research and writing, that these conditions and events ever existed and my alarm that somewhere on this troubled earth the fate of children is ever in crisis.

~1

People had been disappearing. Everyone knew that. And yet, when Alex came down to breakfast and found his whole family had been taken away—his mother, his father, his young sister Nadya, and his old grandmother—he couldn't quite believe it. He hadn't heard a thing because of his crazy room, just a little cell on the second floor that had been used for storage, small, stuffy, with only a tiny window near the ceiling giving dim light. He disliked it heartily because he had to go through his parents' room and then push through all the stored things—old clothes, quilts, boxes—to get to his bed. He had been secretly angry when they had made him move from the room he and Nadya shared, with its window over the garden, so that Nadya could have it all to herself. It had seemed entirely unfair, but he was accustomed to obeying without protest. He had long understood that the rights of children were limited to the wishes of parents.

Now he thought that it was probably the crazy room that had saved him. When the GPU, the secret police, came to take everyone away, they had overlooked the storeroom. Certainly the only good thing about that room was its isolation. One could take one's feelings there and hide them and not be distracted from one's brooding by sounds of people talking, wagons, or trucks rolling on the cobblestones, . . . or gunshots. It was a good retreat, too, for working on the tricky math puzzles that his teacher, Katriana Sergyeva Sokolova, invented for him.

When he had come down to breakfast, there wasn't a sign of anyone; no fire in the grate. There wasn't even the detested smell of scorched oatmeal. But even before that, the first thing that had alerted Alex and started the wave of fear had been the chair overturned in the front hall. His mother, tidy as she was, never would have allowed a chair to remain that way for more than a moment. Her insistence on neatness was why he stood there so early in the morning, well-groomed, brushed, combed, boots polished, to avoid her saying, "Alex, let me see you. Did you lose your brush? That is not the clean shirt that I put out for you. What happened to the shoe wax? Did it evaporate?"

He straightened the chair and called hesitantly, "Mama? Papa?" When there was no answer, he called, "Nadya? Grandmother? Where is everyone?" The chilly house, with its cooling hearth, seemed to answer with an echo, "Nary one," and even as he called, a very cold feeling started in his chest. Tight. Frightened. *It could have happened to them!*

Like birds in winter, snow in spring, people had been disappearing for months, years now, yet none dared talk about it except in the privacy of their homes with the curtains drawn. But Alex knew that certain people and even whole families were being arrested and sent away. Sent where? Why? There were many guesses, but there was no pattern. They only knew it was political, like everything else these days. Since the civil war and the revolution nobody was really safe, yet Alex's father behaved as if they were. He was not political; he did not go to private meetings of revolutionaries or counterrevolutionaries. Still, the civil war had

2

made "enemies" of very ordinary people who had no idea why they had become enemies. Alex's father had told him that much. But he was an educator, the administrator of several schools. It was not a political job—not then, anyhow. He told his teachers not to discuss politics with the students in their classes. It was not their business.

Yes, but then why had they taken away the fat old postmistress one day when she was sorting mail? What could an old woman like that have done? Alex had asked his father, but he had only shrugged. The Levchenko family down the road had been dragged out to a closed van one day, just as Alex was coming home from school—Mr. Levchenko, an engineer, stooped and pale, his wife crying, and the children clinging to her, carrying no possessions. Alex had known Sascha Levchenko very well. His father had said, "Try not to think about it." Alex had tried, but nevertheless it was one of the things he thought about a great deal in his crazy room, away from distracting sounds and activity. Once, a few years ago, his Uncle Dmitri in Moscow had sent him a very shiny stone. "This will turn to gold," he had written, "if you will hold it in your hand and not think of camels." Alex had tried and tried to banish the thought of camels from his mind as he held the stone, but he could not. He could not forget the Levchenkos either, despite his father's advice.

In his little room, he often wondered how life could be so perilous for the people, even though his father had told him that the new government was a "people's government." Still, it was *people* who were taken away or shot, and hundreds, thousands, streamed along the roads at the edge of town, going anywhere, nowhere, made homeless by this people's government. There were months at a time when the town had had no meat, no milk, no bread. The peasants were being forced to give up their farms, their cattle, grain, farm implements, and join collectives. Many of them burned their fields instead. Alex understood that the Czar had been selfish and cruel and that was why there had been a revolution and civil war, but then why wasn't it better now? These were things he thought about.

When he asked his father about that, his father had spoken carefully. "Perhaps it will be better. Do you remember the famine? Even people like us had difficulty getting any food at all, and thousands died of hunger. Now you have oatmeal on the table nearly every morning, don't you? We have a rich soup at night, and sometimes meat. There is bread from the government store most of the time. You would be wiser, Alex, not to think about whether this government is better or worse. If you live your life in an orderly and honest way, be obedient, do your work well, and mind your own business, you will prosper."

"Yes, but Papa, the police come and take the people. . . ."

"Speaking historically," his father had said, "revolutions cause changes. Didn't you read about the French Revolution?"

"People were beheaded!" Alex had cried.

"Yes," his father had replied. "Blood ran in the streets."

"I remember the fighting in the streets here in Kovrov," Alex recalled. "I remember the blood then. I remember . . ."

"Try not to think about it," his father had said. There it was again, the stone that would not turn to gold.

For a while, that particular morning, a shocked and frightened Alex kept walking around and around the house as if he might be able to find his family if he kept going around long enough. Finally, through the fear came the knowledge that he might be in danger himself. In the case of the Levchenkos, a new family had been moved into the house the very same day, a commissioner of the agricultural authority with an office in the town hall. So Alex went back to his crazy room and hastily gathered some things. He had a few kopeks of his own, in a black lacquered box, and he put them in the pocket of his jacket. He put on his warm coat and woolen hat, and, taking his book bag, went through the house closing all the doors. He watered his mother's plant with the red flower in the sunny front window and put out a crust for the birds as he always did. Then he went out and closed the door.

Somehow he felt like a thief, sneaking away from the house with his school bag. He looked up and down the street, felt nobody noticed him, then ran across the road and started over the bridge. At first, he didn't really know where he was going; he just had to get away from the house before the secret police returned or the new tenants moved in.

He passed the great old church with its beautiful blue dome, and, for a moment of precious lapsed memory, he thought he could run in and ask the help of the old priest. But just as quickly the idea was trampled by true recollection of a night a few years ago when soldiers had stormed the church and taken the ikons, candelabra, and chalices. That night, hundreds of the faithful had fought with pitchforks and sticks to try to save the ikons, but they were beaten and the ringleaders sent before a firing squad. After that the church had been closed and the priest taken away and shot. The bells had been melted for cannon balls the year before. The church, now a granary, stood like a holy specter.

Alex's mother had taken over his and Nadya's religious

training. It was permitted that three other children take part in this home instruction, and so his special friend, Grisha, and Grisha's little sister and brother had come to the house once a week to study with them. But there was no mass, no sacraments, no beautiful chants, and his mother was quietly bereaved.

So Alex could not run for sanctuary to the old priest, and, while he did not know what his final destination could be, he knew he could not go anywhere without speaking to Katriana Sergyeva and telling her what had happened. She was not only his teacher, she was a friend of his family. He knew she admired his skill at math, but he felt, too, that she liked him for himself. As for him, he admired her completely. In his eyes, she was truly beautiful, clever, and wise, and he valued her good opinion of him.

How a day can creep! Not move at all! There it sits, a block of time to be cut through slowly with a dull saw. Alex agonized through the school day but was relieved that none of his classmates said anything to him about his family. No one could have seen them go. It must have happened deep in the night. He did not even tell his best friend Grisha. One thing everyone had learned, even before the civil war, was to keep things to oneself. Keep your mouth shut. Don't trust anyone who might betray you to the reds, to the whites, and now to the Bolshevik government. Not Grisha, of course— but words, once spoken, have wings.

Nothing, though, could shake Alex's faith in Katriana Sergyeva, and his impatience to speak to her was like a flea in 'iis shirt as he waited. When the last lesson was finished, he gathered his things and told Grisha not to wait for him.

"I'm staying to do some work," he lied, hating to lie to

Grisha but knowing he must, for his safety and for Grisha's. The less he knew, the better.

"For Katriana, eh, I'll bet," Grisha teased, and poked him. "What do you see in that bag of bones?"

Alex was used to these jibes, so he just returned Grisha's shove and said, "Ah, you're just envious because I beat you in math." He was acting very well, he thought—playful, not worried, while all the day his insides had been crying, moaning, sometimes screaming. It was like pain, but worse.

"I'll come over after supper," Grisha said. "We can walk down to the river and watch them chopping ice. They worked last night with torches."

"No, not tonight," Alex said quickly. Perhaps too quickly, he thought.

"Well, I'll come over and we can play a game of cards," Grisha said, and ran off.

Katriana greeted Alex with her wonderful smile. "I have a special problem for you that I think will take you all night to do," she said.

"May I speak to you, please?" Alex asked. "I don't think I can do a special problem tonight."

"What's the matter, Alex?" Katriana asked. She immediately responded to the serious tone and distressed look.

Now that he had her ear, he didn't know how to begin. "I don't want to involve you," he began. "I would like to . . . I need to ask your advice. My family . . . they've been . . . I think . . . Oh, Katriana Sokolova, *they're gone.*" Spoken, the words became truth. What terrible shape this truth had, enormous, black, ominous. The truth of the morning had been frightening, but blank, shapeless. Now he felt the cold fear all over again, but stronger.

"Oh, Alex! Alex, are you sure?" She quickly rose and closed the classroom door. Then he told her about the morning, swallowing now and then to gulp down the weeping feeling in his throat.

"But they could have gone out on an early errand," Katriana said. "Perhaps they are all back there now waiting for you to come home from school." Kindness mixed with the anxiety in her voice.

For less than a second that thought became a hope, and his fear turned to an urgent desire to run home and see. But in his heart he knew they would never have gone out, all of them, all at once, so early and without telling him. "No," he said to her. "No, I don't think it's possible." And he told her about the cold hearth and the chair.

"But a chair! Anyone could knock over a chair. We mustn't rush to conclusions. Perhaps you should go home, as usual, and see." She had said what Alex had hoped, for just that second, but she, too, quickly saw how impossible that was. "No," she said immediately. "You can't do that." She thought a moment, then rummaged in her bag and gave him a key. "Here's what I think you must do. You know the house I live in. The room is right at the top of the stairs on the third floor. Let yourself in quietly and wait for me. I'll see what I can find out."

"But you could get in trouble!" Alex protested.

"I'll be very careful. Now go quickly."

Tears choked Alex's throat. He knew what she was doing was dangerous, but he did exactly as he was told because he didn't know what else to do. He was twelve years old, but on this day he was so insecure and uncertain that he felt as he had when he was a much younger child.

He climbed the stairs of the old square building only three

8

streets from the school. He didn't think this a proper place for Katriana at all—dull gray, while she was bright and shining. Perhaps, if he were to admit the truth, he would have to say she was not really as beautiful as he thought her to be, but it always surprised him, each time he saw her, to find she was not exactly as he imagined her. She had the kind of beauty that affected people's hearts and fooled their eyes. Her dark golden hair usually flew in disarray from a loose knot atop her head. Her dark bright eyes seemed overlarge in her thin pale face. Perhaps she was, as Grisha said, bony. If so, it became her, Alex thought.

Her room was tiny, without enough light, and yet it was pleasant in its way. He could see that when he had entered and closed the door. The small bed was covered with an old red quilt. Above it was a blue and gold ikon. A green velvet chair stood next to a table that was covered with an elaborately embroidered scarf. On the wall, over the weathered wooden trunk, was a summer scene, a field with a river beyond. Alex sat down and waited, staring deeply into the painting, thinking of summer and walking in the hills with his father's old friend Tolka who lived in the wild, sleeping on the ground, eating berries, with no companions but the wolves. He tried to concentrate on that and not think of the frightening trouble that had beset him. Once again, it was like trying not to think of camels.

It was dark by the time Katriana came in with several things in a basket. Alex was slumped in the chair, napping, and awoke to find her poking at the stove. She started speaking fast as soon as he greeted her.

"I'm sorry you had to wait so long. There was such a long line for bread that I was afraid they would run out of it before I reached the counter, so I did something I have never done before—I paid a homeless waif who was selling places. I could have done that at first and wouldn't have wasted so much time, but I don't like to encourage them to come here. As long as we give them coins or they are able to steal something, they will stay around and plague us by making us feel guilty. I don't know why the government doesn't do something. Oh, I am just saying that, but I know perfectly well that anything the state can do is not enough. All they can do is ignore them or arrest them and punish them for having no homes. There are just too many of them and they are so abysmally in need."

Finally, she sat on the edge of the bed and looked straight into Alex's eyes. "I am prattling on because I don't want to tell you what I must. I'm afraid you are right." Alex could only nod his head. "I walked past your house several times to see if there was any activity. The third time I walked down the street, I saw Grisha coming out of your gate. I pretended to be passing by. I said, 'Good evening, Grisha. All through with your game?' And he said, 'Nobody's home. They must have all gone visiting.' So I waited until dusk and walked past again to see if there were any lights. There are none, Alex. Of course, there is always the chance that they have indeed gone visiting, as Grisha said, or that . . ."

Life seemed to stop. He heard himself say, "No, not at supper hour. Certainly not since morning." He felt as if this were happening to someone else and he were watching it. His voice sounded far-off and muffled in his ears.

"Well, we'll see tomorrow," Katriana said. "Now, try to eat some bread with sausage and a little tea." She poured the hot black tea into little decorated cups and cut the sausage and bread. These she put on the embroidered cloth, and they sat together in the light from the grate. In his most secret dreams, Alex had imagined himself sitting thus with Katriana, though he had never seen the room before. Now it was as if the dream had contained all these details—the embroidered cloth, the trunk, the worn green velvet chair, the picture on the wall. But his dream had been joyous, and this was full of pain.

At first they sat silently, but finally Alex asked, "Why would they take my father? What could he have done?"

"What could any of them have done! The thousands!" Katriana mourned softly. "Your father is a good man, a fine man, but perhaps today that is not enough. The new government will want the students to be taught to think a particular way, as the government thinks. Perhaps your father is too . . . well, neutral, impartial. I have read some government writings about education. The Bolsheviks know that if the idea of communism is to succeed, the children will have to be taught very young to think as they are told to think. Of course, that is one of the purposes of the Komsomol, the youth organization, and many of the children are joining that."

"But my father is very strict," Alex said. "I must always do as he says."

"Perhaps," Katriana replied. "But do you always *think* as he thinks?"

"No," Alex said. "I go to my crazy room and think as I wish to think, and when I am fully grown up I shall be able to do as I wish, as well."

"Yes," Katriana said, smiling. "I hope that is true."

Unlike his old crazy room at home, Katriana's room picked up the noises on the street, the rumble of wagons and vans over the rough cobbles, the calls of children. Then there came a steady drumming of boots on stone, the passing

11

of a patrol of soldiers who were billeted in the old grain warehouse at the edge of town. The citizens had come to accept the soldiers as a part of the new way, but even so, it was disturbing to hear the volleys of shots that rang out during practice hours. It made everyone remember the terrible days of fighting only a few years before, when those shots had struck live bodies, not clay targets. Alex thought of those days as of a bad dream, terrible but not true. Did they really happen?

"We must think about what you must do, Alex," Katriana was saying. "I would like to keep you here with me, but you know I cannot do that for long. Soon it will be known that your family is gone, and then, if you are seen in the town, someone may turn you in. You know that. The town council will praise the Komsomol children for that. They'll send you to an orphanage, and they are quite terrible today, over-crowded with *bezprizorni**—these miserable homeless waifs." She frowned. After a pause she said, "I am thinking of the eyes of that child who held my place in line. They frightened me. They were so fierce. They threatened rather than pleaded. My God, I wish there were something one could do! The government is too busy defending itself to consider children." She turned her attention to the problem at hand once again. "Alex, do you have any relatives in a nearby town?"

"Not nearby. My Uncle Dmitri lives in Moscow, but I haven't seen him since he came here two years ago. The rest of my relatives live far in the east, a thousand miles or more."

---

* the wild children. Literally, shelterless. (See glossary, page 151.)

12

"Perhaps, then, you could go to Moscow to your uncle? Do you know where he lives?"

"He lives just off Tvershaia Street in a house behind a café. We had chocolate and rum cake there once. A man played the balalaika. It was a long time ago, but I remember it."

Katriana's face brightened. "All right, then, tomorrow we will see about sending you to your uncle." She looked at him with her warm dark eyes shining with tears. "Alex, do not give up hope," she said. "Perhaps your family will make contact with him, too, and one day you will be reunited. For now, you must be very strong and think about yourself, your future. I will tell you that I wish I could go away from here myself. There now, I have not confessed that to anyone."

"But where would you go?" He was diverted from his misery, for the moment, by the marvelous fact of becoming her confidant.

"I'm not sure. Across one of the borders to somewhere in Scandinavia, possibly, and then later, perhaps, to Canada or the United States."

"Out of the country! Leave Russia!"

Katriana lowered her voice to a whisper. "It is only a dream, of course. Sooner or later, all the old bourgeois teachers like me, like your father, will be replaced by young proletariats, anyway. We are suspect. Don't think, Alex, that the idea of socialism is bad. It may be good. It is just there are good people and bad people in all systems, and sometimes the good people are overwhelmed by the bad. It is power that is the evil."

"How would you get away?" Alex asked.

Once again, Katriana lowered her voice to a whisper. "My

13

brother, Basil Sergyevitch, is a librarian in the Anitchkoff Palace in St. Petersburg. He had been studying in the seminary to become a priest, but when the seminary was closed he went to work in the library. He is . . . well, political. He has helped many people to leave, one way or another. I know I could go to him. Living frightened is making me old. And frightened of *what*?"

Alex saw now how drawn her thin face was. How sad.

"We don't even know who or what to fear, and so we fear everyone and everything." Katriana continued. "Now, in the deep winter, one can feel the desperation everywhere. First the famine, the war with the Germans, the revolution, Russian against Russian, one's friends disappearing. More famine, people straggling along the roads from other towns, looking for anything to eat. And the thousands of homeless children. This is not *matusa Rus**[*] I have loved. Oppression, whether from the reds or whites, Czar or Bolsheviks, is not bearable. Much as I have loved my homeland, *there must be someplace better*, as things are."

"When would you go?" Alex asked, thinking, hoping she might go now, with him.

"I don't know. This is the first time I have thought so clearly on the matter. I know I cannot leave the children in my class in the middle of the school year, leave them to who knows what kind of teaching. Still, I am going to think about it. I really am." She stopped and clapped her hands over her face. "I am talking too much about myself when you are the one with the sad problem now. Alex, I want you to remember where my brother is, just in case you should ever find you are thinking that way, yourself."

* Mother Russia

14

Alex thought how lovely and real she was in her deepest feelings, just as beautiful as the idol of gilded plaster he had thought her. Now she laid the quilt on the floor for him, and he settled himself on it. She knelt beside him and pulled the quilt over his shoulders, then brushed a cowlick of fair hair off his forehead. "Good night, Alex," she said softly.

"Good night, Katriana Sergyeva."

Was it strange that he fell asleep immediately and did not dream? In those night hours, his waking mind and his sleeping mind fled from truth and into a dark silence of false peace.

~2

When he awoke in the morning, she was gone. There was a note beside a piece of cheese and a chunk of bread. "Stay here out of sight." He spent a dull day in the room, pacing around like a dog on a chain. He read bits of her books, but he couldn't concentrate on the words. Part of his brain read the lines while another part went over the events of the day before, mourned his family, imagined the future with his uncle in Moscow. When he felt it was time for her to return, he started looking out of the window, peering from behind the heavy draperies. Finally, when he had started to worry, she came along the street, carrying her books and her basket and looking over her shoulder. Then, instead of coming into the building, much to Alex's dismay, she passed right by. But soon she reappeared on the other side of the street and, looking about cautiously, crossed the cobbles and quickly entered the building. When she came into the room, she was smiling, carrying a pot of something hot, but Alex could tell she was very tight inside, just as he was.

"Look, Madame Minsky, downstairs, has given me this fine potato soup. Isn't it lovely! She pays me this way for teaching her to read."

"Why did you go by the building? Is somebody following you?"

"No, I'm certain no one is. I am just extra cautious. I am responsible for you. All the same, I think it would be best for you to leave for Moscow as soon as possible. Several of the children have noticed your empty house." She opened her bag and took out a book. "I have brought the atlas from the classroom." She opened it, turning the pages and peering at them closely in the late afternoon light. "See, here is our town of Kovrov and here is Moscow. The direction is almost due west. Tomorrow, you must walk to Vladimir and buy a ticket at the station. I am sure nobody knows when the train stops, of course. They are so irregular these days. But there will be one, sooner or later, and when you get to Moscow, you can ask a hack driver to take you to your uncle's street. You could be there in a single day. Now"—she went to the trunk and opened it, taking out a small leather purse— "here are some rubles I have set aside. They should buy you a ticket and pay for the hack. I will give you some bread and sausage to carry, and you can buy tea at the station. I think you should go as soon as it is light in the morning, so let's have a little soup and we'll go to sleep early."

"But I can't take your money," Alex protested. "You will need it yourself to go away."

"Hush," she commanded. "I am still your teacher, and you must do as I say. Tomorrow, and until you find your uncle, you will make your own decisions." She smiled, and her smile warmed the room and helped to dull the lonely feeling that had beset Alex all day. He knew he must do as she directed. It was the only safe thing to do. And yet, to leave home and to leave this sanctuary all in so short a time was a

17

pain such as he thought he might feel if he were being clawed by wolves and left bleeding in the snow, a nightmare of his childhood.

The walk to Vladimir was one Alex had taken many times before with his father. It was only about six miles, and in good weather it was a pleasant and bracing walk of companionship along roads rich in fir trees, birches, and, in the spring, berry bushes that begged the traveler to slow down and eat. Not this day. Snow beginning to drift along the roads made the walk long and slow. He tried to walk in the cart tracks, but this early in the morning not many carts had passed, and the lightly falling snow covered them. Still, he was warmly dressed, and, long before daylight, Katriana had given him a breakfast of hot tea and something rare and precious, an egg. She had packed him sausage and bread, and he had put it in his school bag. She, herself, had wrapped his scarf closely around his neck, covering his chin, pulling his cap down over his forehead and ears. When she put her arm about him in farewell, he had returned her embrace, clinging, loath to leave her, her friendship, her kindness, the only person left in Kovrov he could trust. Then she had given him a gentle push, a few soft words of encouragement, warning, hope. "*Dasvedanya,** Alex," she had said at last. "Not good-bye, but until we meet again."

"*Dasvedanya,*" he had said. "*Dasvedanya,* Katriana Sergyeva."

His feet tramping in the snow kept that rhythm, and his heart cried it as he walked. "*Dasvedanya* Katriana, *dasvedanya* Katriana . . ." The birches, friends of spring and

* farewell

18

summer, now threw down upon him clots of snow that had settled on their branches, overweighting them. He tried to follow Katriana's advice and not dwell on what had happened, and tried to direct his thoughts ahead to what would be. He thought of the city as he remembered it, softly lit at night, people laughing in the restaurants, and the warm, book-lined walls of his uncle's house where he lived alone. He worked for a newspaper—Alex knew that—and wrote articles and little booklets. Once he had helped Alex write a story for school about his trip to Moscow. He had fixed up the misspelled words and punctuation, but he had said it was good, very good. Alex might like to be a writer, too, he said, when he grew up. Perhaps, Alex thought, he will teach me to be a writer now.

And then he was at the station. The roads, with only stragglers in small groups at this early hour, gave him no hint that the station would be mobbed. People were sprawled everywhere—on the floors, on the benches, on top of baggage and mail bags. Some slept upright, leaning against walls. Alex pushed his way through the maze of sleeping bodies, eliciting a grunt here, a moan there, getting a kick or two in the process. At the ticket window he saw that the stationmaster was asleep, too. Alex cleared his throat. He knocked. Nothing. Finally, he reached through the opening and tapped the gnarled hands lying relaxed and weary upon the desk. The old man jumped and then regarded Alex through the slits of his draped eyes. "Yes, yes! What is it?"

"A ticket to Moscow, if you please," Alex said.

"You woke me for that!"

"I'm sorry. But how else can I buy a ticket?"

"A ticket, a *ticket*! What is needed is a *train*. Don't you see

19

these people? They have been waiting since Tuesday. The train is two days late. There's no hurry for a ticket, but since you are here and I have been awakened anyhow, I will sell you a ticket."

Holding the ticket, Alex felt he was well on his way to Moscow and looked around for a place to set down his school bag and rest until the train came. What he was regarding was a solid carpet of human beings so mixed up that it was hard to tell which feet belonged to which body. But in the dark corner he saw a high pile of sacks, and, in the shadowy light of the station, he proceeded to clamber upon the sacks to find a spot on which he could settle. Suddenly he felt a sharp pain in his leg. Had he been bitten? A rat? But in the next moment the sacks became animated, and something cried out. A face appeared, and then another and another. Then, before his eyes, nearly half the pile of sacks arose and became filthy boys, clad in rags, their crusted, sooty faces scowling and snarling as they unraveled themselves from each other.

"*Svolotch!*"*

"*Dryan!*"**

"Do you have so much to eat that you can't wait to wake up and eat it?" shouted the sack that Alex had stepped on, and he gave Alex a push that sent him sprawling onto the station floor, his fall broken by yet another sleeping body that awoke to shout at him and strike him. He protected his head with his school bag, which had stayed with him because the strap was slung around his neck.

"I'm sorry," he called above the uproar. "I didn't see you."

* swine
** selfish bastard

"What are you, blind?" his assailant challenged.

"Shut up, shut up!" the cries came from around the station. "Let some people sleep. Is there so much else to do? Has the train come, at last, after three days?"

Now the tiny old stationmaster came from behind his desk. He was carrying an enormous pole with a hook on the end. "Any trouble and I have instructions from the local soviet to put this through the stomach of the troublemaker." He waved it toward Alex and then toward the ragged boy, and the boy melted back into the sacks, which were now squirming and coughing, readjusting themselves.

Alex remained where he had fallen, his head near someone else's boots, his shoes close to someone's head. He did not fall asleep, despite his fatigue, but lay awake hearing the coughs, moans, snores, wheezes about him, which gathered into a mass of sound like an impending storm. Yet he must have fallen asleep at some point, because all of a sudden the bodies were moving, arising quickly, gathering belongings and rushing toward the platform. And yes, there it was, slowly chugging and clanging into the station, the old steam engine and the rackety carriages finally hissing to a halt.

Then, as if the station were not already crowded enough, people on the train poured out to stretch their legs, to buy tea from vendors who had materialized from the crowd. Alex reached for his school bag to get some bread, thinking to buy some tea and warm himself. *Gone!* A piece of strap still lay on his shoulder. The rest was cut. A moment of panic and terror, tears close to his eyes, his throat. Alone, and now with nothing to eat! What could he do? He felt in his pocket. A few coins remained with his ticket. He must conserve them. No tea. No bread.

21

The bundles of rags had rematerialized into incredibly dirty and shabby boys who now spread out and mingled with the crowd from the train. Some, the littlest, were begging outright.

"Don't give him anything, Papa," a young passenger said. "He's rude and dirty." Whereupon the urchin spat upon the child, and the father reached out for the waif with his walking stick, missing. The waif laughed at him.

"Here," a nicely dressed woman said, "give them these crusts from our luncheon. But make them say thank you. They must learn some manners if they are to advance at all."

Several of the urchins were standing one on the other's shoulders, the topmost reaching into the open windows of some of the carriages, taking whatever they could reach. A woman screamed, "Watch everything or those dreadful children will snatch it!"

The *peryzronok*° rang. It meant there were five minutes to board. Alex went to a second-class carriage and tried to push himself into the boarding crowd. People jostled for position, trying to be first aboard to claim the few remaining places. Alex allowed himself to be elbowed back numerous times as a woman with a child pushed him gently or a large man pushed him not too gently out of the way. Meanwhile he watched the first-class passengers leisurely exercising themselves, chatting, drinking their tea from their own china cups. Where were they coming from so nicely dressed, and where were they going to? he wondered. Many soldiers in uniforms paced up and down or escorted ladies on their

° one ring of the railroad bell

arms. The *tretyzvonok*° rang and they started for their carriage, unrushed.

The urchins stood on the side, imitating the strolling of the first-class passengers, smirking at them and at each other, laughing, smoking, punching one another about. The guards were going along the outside of the whole train with batons, beating at the space beneath the train and chasing children who were attempting to ride beneath the carriages, but they would no sooner leave one spot than the children would race back again.

Now, in a last surge of the crowd, Alex found himself aboard, crowded like a sprat near the steps of the carriage and not able to sit down. Indeed, he hardly needed to stand on his feet because the crowd pressed him so closely. The wooden seats of the carriage were jammed with peasants in the typical *muzik*°° costume—blue cloth trousers thrust into boots, stiff jackets, and the proletarian cap with sharp visor stuck on the back of the head. There were farmers with their combed red beards, women in shawls, carrying swaddled infants. They all sat surrounded with bundles. The noise and the odors of the car were strong, and Alex thought he had never been so uncomfortable. But, he thought, it will only be a few hours and I will be in Moscow. I can bear being hungry until then, and I guess I can stand being uncomfortable that long, he thought as the train picked up speed.

He was not to find that out. The train came to a sudden stop. Some of the people seated in the wooden benches fell

° three rings of the bell to indicate that the train is about to leave
°° peasant

forward, crying out. Alex, packed as he was, was hardly jarred. Now the door of the car was thrown open by the guard. "Out!" he ordered to the crowd around Alex. "Everyone standing in this corridor, out." In a few minutes, Alex was standing on the road at the verge of the rail line, watching a group of soldiers mounting the cars in their stead.

"But we have paid for tickets," several people cried to the guard.

"Too bad," the guard said. "The soldiers come first. You can wait here for the next train. The engineer will stop if he sees you."

"*If* he sees us! *If* there's room! *If* it comes!" one man shouted, shaking his fist.

"We'll have to walk," Alex heard a man say to his wife, who was carrying a child. "The next train may not be for days, and the child will have starved by then."

The train was out of sight now, leaving only a trail of steam and smoke to show them where it had been.

"How can I walk to Moscow?" the woman with the baby asked her husband. "It must be a hundred miles and I have no heavy boots for the snow."

The man was kind. "What are the choices? Shall we stay here and starve? Do you see anyone coming with food for us and the child? Every step we take is that much closer to your cousin in Moscow and that much closer to food. Hold that thought. Come."

Alex thought the man might be talking to him, as well. It's true, he thought to himself. What will happen if I stay here? Perhaps I had best go back to Kovrov and ask Katriana. But Katriana had already told him he was not safe at home and he knew that. He found himself following the man and his wife and child and several others who had been standing there at a loss.

If they could have looked down upon themselves from the height of a cloud, they would have seen that they were just a wave, a small one, in a large ocean of people along the roads to Moscow: people in wagons, people in sleds, people carrying people, but mostly people on their own two feet, dragging themselves by force toward something better—something less bad, at least—than they were leaving. From the known to the unknown.

At first Alex tried to pretend that he was on a great adventure to a foreign land, a pioneer, a crusader, an explorer, a discoverer. Beyond the unknown roads, hills, snowy crests, lay a new but exciting world in which he might be one of the first to set foot. There would be cold, hunger, even wolves to combat, but the new land that he would find would be such a kind and abundant land that it would be worth it. He would be among the rulers because he would be there first. What rules would he make? One thing he knew he would do. He would find his parents and his sister and grandmother. That he knew certainly. He played with this idea, off and on, for hours, stopping now and then to take a mouthful of clean snow as he saw the others do. Now their number seemed to have increased. Out of the small roads, others had been drifting, like the snow itself, into the straggly line, and the snow blanket deadened the sound of their journey, dulled the sound of the babies crying, of small children announcing their hunger, old people groaning under the weight of their bundles and their bodies.

Who led this band? Alex did not know. He was following

an unseen leader, trusting he was going in the right direction. In the distance could be seen the white palaces and green- and gold-domed churches of Nijni-Novgorod. Dark pines stood out against the sky on the hill of the upper city, separated from the lower city by the great Volga. Alex knew where he was. Once, when he was a little boy, his father had taken him and his mother to the fair at Nijni-Novgorod. It still shone in his memory, like the trip to Moscow.

The ice-glazed setting sun assured him he was indeed headed west, toward Moscow. He thought this may, have been the longest day of his life. It seemed impossible that only early this morning he had left Katriana in her little room in Kovrov. It seemed, now, a lifetime away.

As night fell, Alex settled himself within his coat in the shelter of a half-destroyed wall. He ate more snow and rubbed his feet vigorously before he fell into an exhausted sleep. If he dreamed, the dreams did not linger. He was blessedly unconscious in the black world where there was no hunger.

It was incredible chill that awoke him finally, pulling him from the protection of sleep. His body was quaking with cold, and he could hardly find his feet. When he stood, they just barely supported him, but after he had stumbled about a bit he was better, painful but stable. He saw the couple whom he had followed from the station. They had built a small fire of trash in the snow and were holding the baby over it as if toasting it. At the same time, the woman was dipping her handkerchief in the snow and letting the baby suck on it.

"We are going now," she said, addressing Alex. "You can try and warm yourself on what is left of this little fire, if you wish." It occurred to him now that he had spoken to nobody during this journey and nobody had spoken to him. They all seemed to have been traveling separately in their own small world of trouble. It was as though, if one spoke, one might lose what little one still had, one's sense of one's self.

Alex nodded his thanks, sat down, and took off his boots. He put his feet nearly into the fire. He tried to envelop the fire with his body. Then, taking a cue from the woman, he filled his kerchief with snow and chewed it. The act of chewing gave him the illusion of eating.

It seemed that now their ranks had swelled until they choked the narrow roads. There were many young boys and a few girls among the travelers, traveling alone or in groups. They bore more of a resemblance to the mob at the station than they did to him. Finally, he got the courage to speak. "How long have you been walking?" he asked a very ragged boy who was trudging nearby.

The boy stared at Alex, regarding his heavy clothing and replying in a deep grunting croak. "Three, four months."

"Months!" Alex cried. "Did you say *months?*"

"You'll see." The boy laughed with a sort of disgusted snarl, and he fell back to await a companion.

Along the road were fallen telegraph poles and tangles of wires. *Muziks* were hacking at the poles for fuel. Around the snowy fields stood the remains of burned farmhouses. They passed the ruins of a fine manor—six great pillars, with a rubble of stone surrounding them. By midday, Alex was so tired that he had to rest. He sat by the side of the road and watched people stumbling along. His eyes closed.

Then someone was shaking him. "Don't sleep too long, child," a woman's harsh voice said. "You'll freeze. There's a wicked wind here. Get up and move if you have any sense."

But she did not stay to see if he did. Alex pulled himself to his feet. He felt light-headed, almost absent. He did not know where the rest of that day went. He floated along in a body that did not belong to him, and, when it was too dark to walk further, he entered what was left of a vandalized church. The benches had been removed, the ikons were gone. Garbage and rags were in piles. People lay among them, indistinguishable from them. Alex collapsed beside a stone wall, sheltered at least from the wind. There, surrounded by dispossessed ghosts of saints and martyrs, he slept.

~3

The snow had stopped, but the wind was even more bitter. Mistletoe and willows, so lovely in spring, looked threatening and black. Alex tried not to think of soup. He tried not to think of the warmth of it as it hits the face when one leans over the bowl, of the great hot slices of potato, carrots, beans, cabbage, and rich chunks of meat that first encounter the taste buds, become masticated by sharp teeth, and pass down the throat into the stomach, warming the throat, the gullet, and the belly. He began counting steps—two hundred, two hundred and ten, two hundred and fifty—but always the vision of the soup came back, floating like a phantom just in front of him, out of reach. Now it was joined by a vision of bread—thick, crusty, laden with soft yellow butter. He recited his multiplication tables, concentrating very hard on the elevens and twelves, always difficult and now, in his weakened state, nearly impossible. But still the soup appeared, and the bread, and now cake and fruit as well. Apples and summer fruits, plums and melons. A samovar of boiling hot water appeared, and fragrant pots of black tea.

The images were strong. He gave up trying to divert himself and tried to imagine their taste. Saliva flowed in his dry mouth, and his stomach contracted with pain as he swallowed. His head felt strangely large and tight, and yet empty, weightless. His body was chilled, but it did not pain him because his attention was focused only on his feet, the deep and terrible cold of them as he tramped through the packed snow, and the fact that they must be kept moving— left foot, right foot, left foot, right foot—until they brought him to the city.

Now he, like the others, became wrapped only in his own misery and, for the most part, remained aloof from the other travelers. But along the sides of the road, he could not avoid the sight of bodies of other children and adults who had not been able to keep their feet moving. At first he had stopped and prodded them, saying, as the woman had said to him, "Come on, get up. You'll freeze that way." But the first child had only moaned, and Alex had been unable to move him. The second did not moan at all. One had used his remaining strength to say, "Go away. Go away." After that Alex tried not to see the bodies along the side of the road. Snow drifting over them helped to blur their reality.

Did he sleep as he walked? He seemed sometimes to return to the road from someplace he had been in his mind, or no place. Now he returned to his body on the road and found that there were dilapidated buildings beside the road, becoming more dense as he progressed. People beside him were saying, "Moscow! This is Moscow!" Alex looked up, and in the distance he could see the sun shining on the many colored domes, blue, green, gold—a dream of heaven. Yes, it must be a dream because around him, here on the road, the same sun seemed cold as the wind blew in great gusts. He drew his wet collar up and put his head down, withdrawing like a tortoise. No, he thought, this can't be Moscow. Besides, all that really mattered now was the cold. He used to think, when he went into the winter woods with old Tolka,

30

that that was as cold as it was possible to be. But Tolka was always able to make a fire out of nothing . . . out of snow, it seemed, if need be.

Soon the tattered buildings beside the road clustered closer and taller—shops and houses with windows barred and broken, mended with rags, tin, and paper, doors hanging on hinges. And, in a while, the road on which he was walking intersected crossroads and then ran into a square with a small market and a few stalls. A woman in peasant clothes held a heavy tray on straps around her neck and was selling threads of many colors. At a nearby stall there was an apple vendor with half a dozen apples, brown and dented, but Alex would have devoured them all if he could. He approached the vendor, reaching into the depths of his inner pocket with his frozen hands to bring forth his tiny store of kopeks. "Please," he said. The vendor surveyed the coins in Alex's hand.

"Not enough," he said.

"But I have not eaten in three days," Alex said.

"Can I give apples away to everyone who has not eaten in three days? No," said the vendor, and turned away.

Alex turned to the woman with the spools of thread. "Can you tell me the way to Tvershaia Street?"

She drew her threads closer and protected them. "I know the way from here to my bed," she said. "Ask a soldier." And she pointed to one of a number of uniformed men who walked casually around the square.

Since the civil war, Alex had had a deep fear of soldiers, men who could shoot each other, who came in the night and carried off friends. So he lingered around the edges of the square in the shadow of a building, not able to muster his courage to approach one. And then suddenly he felt a hand on his shoulder. He wheeled and found himself looking up into the face of just such a uniformed man.

"What are you doing here, eh? Waiting for your chance to rob one of those poor comrade vendors, I'm sure. Well, there will be slim pickings today. From whom did you steal that good coat?" he asked, pulling at the collar. "And the hat? Well, you'd better come with me, now, to the children's detention center."

"No, no!" Alex cried. "I am not a thief."

The young soldier laughed. "Do you think I expect you to say you are?" His voice hardened. "Come on. Let's not waste time. You're not the only waif I have to cart over there today, though I don't know why. There's hardly room for another rat, let alone more *bezprizorni*."

"But listen, I have just come all the way from Kovrov. I have traveled for many days. I am trying to find my uncle near Tvershaia Street. Ask these people," and he pointed to the vendors. "I have been trying to buy an apple, but I haven't enough money. I have asked this old woman the way to Tvershaia Street."

The soldier let go of his collar. "Is that the truth, then? Well, I'll let you go this time. Tvershaia Street is not far from the Kremlin.* Look over that way and you will see the many towers. Go across the next street to the right all the way to the end. Then turn left, up the hill, across the big square, and there you are. Go on now, and don't let me see you back here or I will know you were lying. And you know what we do with liars!"

* former palace of the Grand Duke and Czars, now the center of Soviet government.

Alex tried not to think. He turned and ran. He did not know how he mustered the strength to do it. He had felt, only a moment ago, that he could hardly walk another step. He stumbled across the square and, following the soldier's directions, down the next street to the end, turned left, labored up the hill and to the outskirts of Red Square with a high wall of the Kremlin beyond. The great arches were destroyed and lay in piles of rubble. A scaffolding was erected around the spires of St. Basil's Cathedral. The enormous square seemed almost empty except for a few people on foot and a couple of carts with wooden wheels being drawn, not by horses, but by peasants.

Now he turned, as directed, and soon found himself on Tvershaia Street. He was flooded with new life, hope. The fear, horror, misery of the last few days faded in the expectation of seeing his uncle, embracing him, being welcomed into his warm home. Yes, there was the restaurant where they had had the hot chocolate and rum cakes, in another lifetime, boarded up now. And this was the little street where his uncle's house stood. Yes, there it was. He knew he would recognize the house because of the rosette chiseled in stone over the front door. Suddenly exhausted, he sat for a moment on the stone steps before mounting them. Then, with a resurgence of the kind of tidiness his mother had insisted upon, he reached into the snow and took a scoop into his hand and washed his face, then his hands. He found cleaner snow underneath and took it into his mouth, then spat it out. He took off his wet cap and smoothed his hair. He tried to brush his soiled coat. Then he rose and climbed the steps, his heart beating fast. He pulled the bell.

At first there was no answer, so he pulled it again. Finally the door was opened by an old woman, her hair flying from under a *babushka**, her body swathed in heavy skirts and shawls. She stood shivering in the doorway.

"Hurry up. What is it? We don't want to freeze anymore than we are."

"Good morning, madame. My uncle, Dmitri Antonovich Protopov. I am here to see him."

"I don't know a Dmitri Antonovich," the woman said, trying to close the door, but Alex was standing in the opening.

"I beg your pardon, but he has always lived here. This is his house. He is a journalist. Surely you must know that."

"The only thing I know is that you are making me keep the door open and it is chilling the house that is already so cold we can't breathe. This house belongs to no citizen. It belongs to the people. Six families live in here now, and none of them is named Protopov. Perhaps it was his house, but it isn't now."

"Then where can I look for him? Where has he gone? I have come all the way from Kovrov to see him. He is my only relative within a thousand miles of here." Alex's voice rose in fear and anxiety. He was grasping the woman's arm. She softened her look a bit and cast a nervous glance over her shoulder. Then she raised her voice.

"That's too bad for you, but that's not news. The city is full of children like you, hordes of them." She lowered her voice to a whisper then. "Your uncle was taken away a month ago. You could go to the local soviet and inquire, but I don't think it would be wise." Then she raised her voice again. "I'm sorry, I can't help you," and she gave Alex a little push and he was back on the outside of the closed door.

* scarf

34

He wandered down the steps and slowly back to the corner of the square. A light snow was falling, covering the old drifts with fresh white. It did not look colder than Alex felt. The pain of hunger and cold was now mixed with this new intolerable knowledge—he was alone.

The weakness he felt made him wish to rest for a long time, anywhere. In the snow, if he must. He leaned against a building and, through half-closed lids, regarded the square. He had found, long ago, that squinting made things less real, and he did it now without thinking.

Like the first square, this square had a small market in progress, and peddlers with trays around their necks wandered about, approaching pedestrians. There were several covered barrows with a motley assortment of moldy-looking potatoes, cabbages, turnips, apples. There was a stand of sausages, too, but Alex now felt ill when he thought of them. Around the square stood many shops, but their shattered windows were barred or plugged with rags, their doors boarded up. A city exhausted after a long siege. Soldiers with rifles patrolled the street, and, even through his half-closed lids, Alex could read signs and banners that hung upon the building. "We Are Building a Society." "Religion is Opium for the People." "We Must Make Sacrifices." "We Are Surrounded by Enemies." A large picture of Lenin was hung on the building directly across from him.

Suddenly, like a flight of birds, a pack of children swooped from an alley behind him. Without pause, they descended on the vegetable stall and, in what seemed a single motion, nearly cleared it of its few bits of produce. Then they flew past and were out of sight. The old vendor cried out like a fox shot in one leg, high-pitched, keening. His stall was nearly bare now, as if there had never been any produce at all. Other people standing around shook their heads and shrugged their shoulders. Had they seen the thieves, or was it a ghostly horde conjured by the sun on the snow? They went back to their business of hawking their small stocks or continued their progress through the square.

Now, from the same alley, there crept a very small figure of a boy, ragged, filthy, his clothes flapping about him, his feet bound in rags. Then suddenly, like the others, he broke into a run, passed the vegetable stand, grabbed a remaining cabbage, and, as the owner of the stand renewed his screams, ran behind another stand and ducked out of sight under a barrow. But Alex could see one of his bound feet sticking out, looking like dirty snow or trash.

"Where did he go, the thief?" shouted the peddler. He appealed to Alex. "You. You were standing right there. Where did he go? Which way?"

A soldier patrolling the square spoke sharply to him. "You, boy! Did you see? Where did the filthy rascal go?" He said it angrily, but it was as if he had said the same thing many times before, performing his hopeless duty. Behind the soldier, Alex could see foot withdraw under the stall and the boy move swiftly down the alley.

"That way," Alex croaked, his voice frozen in his throat. "He went that way," and he pointed across the square in the opposite direction.

The soldier took off, but without much vigor, and the peddler muttered, "He's wasting his time. He knows it. We know it. They are like fish in a net full of holes. The question is not, will he catch him; the question is, who is to starve first, we or they?" And he pushed his few turnips and beetroots closer together and brooded them like a mother hen.

"You'd better be careful not to make too much of a fuss," another peddler advised the old man. "They may take their revenge on you."

Now, near the place where the child had been hiding, Alex saw a tall, dark boy appear. He stared at Alex, then signaled him. Alex hesitated, but then moved toward him, the wind blowing through his clothing, his nose brittle in the cold, his body chilled and shaking inside his damp coat. And yet, this boy he now faced wore only a ragged jacket, torn cotton trousers, and an ordinary workman's cap, pulled low over his rugged, wide face. Rag-wrapped feet protruded from the holes in outsize boots, the leather in shreds.

"Why didn't you rat on the boy?" he challenged. Alex drew back and shook his head.

"I don't know. He was so small and so . . ."

"So hungry," the tall boy said, almost angrily. "Well, everyone is hungry. Oh, perhaps not you," he added almost sarcastically, "you with your heavy coat and strong boots and warm cap. Perhaps you have a good home and warm fire and food."

"No," Alex said, and his weariness made him close to tears when he thought of the luxuries the boy had just listed. "I used to have. Now I have no home and no fire. I have not eaten in three days." He felt weak and grabbed the nearest barrow for support.

"Hands away!" shouted the peddler.

"Then, fool, why don't you sell your coat before it is stolen?" the boy asked. "Before I steal it, in fact!" And he laughed a hearty laugh. "Are you with a band?" he asked.

"Band?" Alex asked dully. "I don't know what you mean. I've just arrived in Moscow. I've come to find my uncle, but right now I don't know what to do."

37

"Everyone knows what to do—look for food and shelter. What else would you do?" the boy said.

"But where?" Alex asked.

"You really are green, aren't you?" the boy said. He looked Alex over carefully. "Let me look at your eyes," he commanded. "Open your mouth. Do you spit blood when you cough?" Alex shook his head. "If you are lying, we will beat you up, you know. All right, if you are hungry, you can come with me. What do they call you? I'm Peter."

"Alex," he answered. The boy's rough appearance and manner frightened him, but the invitation to food was too much to resist. And there was something about the boy, through the dirt, through the hard look, that impressed him. He had an authority that was almost like . . . almost like a father's. And with this thought of family, Alex felt the pain sharply again. *Where are they? Will we ever see each other again?*

Peter turned, without another word, and started through the alley, turned left into another alley, out onto streets of boarded buildings, plastered with signs, these shouting curses at England, France, and Italy. They climbed over piles of snow-covered rubble, and finally, after looking cautiously about, Alex followed Peter down stone steps into the cellar of a building that looked as if it could not stand another day, boarded up, broken; surely no one could live here. Down the dark steps they went, along a black corridor to the back, and then, as Peter removed some boards from a wall, into a world such as Alex had never seen, never dreamed existed.

~4

A large cellar with a dirt floor was the place in which he found himself, when he could see at all. The room was filled with a dense oily smoke, lit eerily from the back as if by matches behind a filmy curtain. These lights proved to be several small, smoky fires made of refuse, paper, and rags. When Alex's eyes adjusted he could see that there were many children grouped around each fire, talking, laughing, joking, quarreling, singing, smoking, playing cards. In one corner, a loud fight was going on, and, from the sounds issuing from it, someone was being hurt. Alex could not guess how many occupants there were because, in the dim light and smoke, he could not see the whole area, but everywhere he looked another ragged figure appeared, even in the walls in which there were small hollows like shelves.

Some called a greeting to Peter when they saw him, and he squatted by one of the fires, reaching his hands out to its feeble heat and rubbing them on his face. He took off his wet and torn boots and put his rag-wrapped feet close to the fire; then he motioned Alex to sit.

"This one is named Alex," he said. "Give him a piece of bread and some hot water," he directed one of the boys.

The boy spat. "Why him?" he protested. "You said no bread until supper."

"This will be his supper portion," Peter said sternly, giving the boy a hard look. "He hasn't eaten for three days." The complaining one grunted and shuffled over to a corner where a bag of rags hung from a beam. In a moment, he was back and threw Alex a small piece of stale bread. Alex ate it eagerly, nodding his thanks. Then he drank hot water from a wooden bowl, and he thought he had never experienced such comfort as that as it warmed his throat and stomach.

"That one is Boris," Peter said. "He's in charge of food today. And this is Kostia," he said, pointing to a sharp-faced boy. "Sometimes we call him The Dancer because he walks and dances in his sleep. That clown is Ivan." He pointed to a boy with a round pudding face and no nose to speak of. The boy acknowledged the introduction by crossing his eyes and saluting with the arm of a very pale boy who sat in front of him. "The albino is Leon, and this is Miska," he said, as the small boy Alex had seen at the square came and stood across the fire from them. Peter stood up and walked over to him. He took him by the ear. "What did you think you were doing in the market, you numbskull?" He shook the little boy, and the boy cried out pitifully.

"Peter, don't! I just wanted to earn my share like the others."

"You earn your share by staying here and keeping a fire lit. You can earn your share with the rest of the little ones by begging or juggling. What do you think would happen if you were caught, eh? We'd all be caught and you've been told that a hundred times. Would you like them to take you to the children's home on Pokrovskaia Street? Or perhaps you prefer the one in the Khamovnik Quarter? That one is even worse than the one we were in, in the south. When you are big enough to learn to steal, I will show you how and you will be the best thief in Moscow, but not now." Peter shook him again. "Do you understand? Say you understand."

"I understand."

"Say it again," and he shook the boy once more.

"I understand."

"To make sure you understand, there will be no bread for you tonight. You have contributed your share to Alex for saving you from the soldier." He dropped little Miska to the floor.

"But Peter," Miska whimpered, "I brought a cabbage."

"Good. No cabbage either."

Cabbage! Yes, Alex could distinguish through the many heavy, rancid, nauseating odors of the cellar the unmistakable smell of that beloved vegetable cooking. And it was, in a large pot on the largest of the fires. Exhaustion swept over him now. He took off his boots and tried to warm his toes, and as the terrible sharp edge of the cold subsided, sleep came and slumped him forward.

He was awakened by a shove on his shoulder. It was the small boy Miska holding a wooden bowl of steaming, watery cabbage brew. "Peter said to give you this." His face was mournful. "But you had your share of bread." Alex took it, nodding a thank you to the boy who continued to stand there, gnawing his filthy fingers, watching seriously as Alex drank from the bowl. It tasted terrible, and Alex gagged, nearly vomited. But it was hot and it was nourishing, and the days of walking with hunger and cold had made a difference. He thought of the time—could it be only a few days ago?—when he might have pushed his oatmeal away if it

41

tasted a bit scorched, something that happened often when his old grandmother fixed the breakfast. She was forgetful, his mother had said.

"I got some of the cabbage," Miska said as he watched Alex down the hot broth.

"Yes, I know," Alex replied. "It's very good." And then he remembered that this frail child was to have none.

"Here, have what is left of mine," he offered. He raised the bowl, and suddenly a strong arm struck the bowl and its contents across the dirt floor.

"If I say he gets no soup, he gets no soup," said Peter angrily. "If you are staying here, you must know that what I say is the law."

"But I am not staying here," Alex cried, alarmed at the idea. "I'm not . . . I'm not a . . ."

"You're not what, you *sooksin?*"* Peter challenged, coming close. "You're not hungry? You're not cold? You are not alone with no place to stay? Do you think you are better than we because you have a coat?"

"We could have coats, too," Kostia said, his thin body looking as if the weight of a coat would collapse it. He was putting a spoon into the band of his cap, having just finished his soup. "If we get a coat, we sell it."

"You'd rather be cold?" Alex asked, curiosity outweighing fear. These boys, who had seemed merely filthy and impudent, now seemed more sinister and threatening, their voices hostile. In the light of the fire their gnome-like faces and shaggy, matted hair made them seem like characters in nightmares, or illustrations of evil spirits, seen as they were in the strange oily light.

* son of a bitch

"We would rather," Kostia said, "be warm with full stomachs, but we don't get everything we want."

"Not *everything*!" said Ivan, the clown, fashioning another cross-eyed look. "Of course, we have *most* luxuries!" And he lounged back against one of the other boys, who let him fall to the ground.

"We can keep each other warm better than overcoats do," Kostia said. "Overcoats get wet. But we don't eat each other . . . not yet, anyway." He gave a hard laugh, and the children who heard him tittered without much mirth.

"Well, I will be going in the morning," Alex said.

"Suit yourself," Peter replied. "Nobody has to stay with us. In fact, it is not easy to belong to our band. We have rules."

"What rules?" Alex asked.

"You don't need to know them since you are not staying with us," Peter said. "But it is just as serious as the Komsomol in some ways."

"But you don't have to jump on command," Leon said, "nor go on parade for the people who stole your parents' farm."

"Nor betray your parents," Kostia added, "if you have any."

"The *bezprizorni* are like animals of nature," Peter said. "Perhaps they are cold as dogs in the snow and as hungry as wolves in the forest, but they are free."

Kostia now went to the fire, and, reaching in for a dead coal, he bent over and started to use it to blacken his skin where it was exposed by a rent in his trouser leg.

"Do me, too, Kostia," Miska said, and leaned over while Kostia blackened a spot on the seat of his pants. Some of the smaller children lined up behind Miska to be groomed with coal. Sitting by the fire, Alex watched them, jumping about and playing as if it were a game at school.

43

In a corner nearby, Boris, the custodian of food, and another boy, who Alex remembered had been introduced as Grigory, were quietly setting a fire between the toes of a sleeping boy. Alex wanted to cry out, but the boy wakened in a moment, yowled, and thrashed out the fire. Then he came over and punched Boris and Grigory, and now a small fight was going on.

Throughout the cellar there was some singing. No song was clear, and several songs went on at once, along with much coughing and some shouting. It was clamorous.

Now Miska came and crouched near the fire. He took a tattered red-covered book from under his shirt and turned the pages, studying the finely etched pictures.

"What are you reading?" Alex asked.

"I don't know," Miska said. "I can't read. Peter found it in a real house and gave it to me. I gave Boris and Grigory the thin paper over the pictures for cigarettes."

"Does Peter read it to you, then?"

"Oh, Peter can't read much, either. He was brought up in a children's home, and they do not teach you to read there."

Alex could not believe that. Peter must be fourteen or fifteen. "Here," he said. "Let me see it. I'll read you a bit. Oh, everyone knows this story. My grandmother used to read it to me long ago." And he began to read about the *leshii*, a spirit with great bulbous eyes, long hair, and blue-tinged skin. This spirit was the protector of rascals and thieves. He was a carefree spirit, and it is his sound we hear in the mountains in the echo. If you wander in the woods, he is likely to show you the wrong way home, and you will be lost unless you take off your coat and wear it wrong side 'round.

As Alex read the old tale, he remembered how it was to be curled up against his grandmother, the sweet smell of laven-

44

der on her clothes. Before long, his eyes felt heavy in the
dim light, and he looked up from the book. Miska had fallen
asleep, his head against Alex's shoulder, and around him
were several other rapt listeners regarding him with awe.
From the other side of the fire, Peter was looking at him
thoughtfully. Then, without saying anything, he rolled over
and went to sleep.

The room was quieting. There were whispers from this
corner, wisps of smoke from that one, a hard laugh here, and
intermittent coughing everywhere. But finally, Alex slept,
too. He awoke during the night and found Miska was curled
against him, and so was another boy on the other side. He
settled back again with these ragged live blankets around
him. In the dim light he could see that all the boys were in
piles like bundles of trash and that he had become part of
the huddle, a ragbag of humanity, giving each other the
only thing they had—the little warmth of their bodies.

~5

In the morning the fires were started again, the smoke choking and malodorous. Although Peter's rules demanded that
they leave the cellar to perform bodily functions outdoors,
the place seemed to reek of excrement. Pots of water were
set to boil, and in a while there was a bowl of hot water for
each and a piece of bread the size, Alex thought, of a crust
he might leave on his plate in the morning or toss to the
birds. Today was Kostia's turn to be in charge of food, and
he measured out each piece carefully, feeling the respon-
sibility of his charge. He would guard the cache all day to
be sure there were no rule-breakers.

Now Alex could see there were a pair of finches in the
cellar with them, flying about, dining on hemp seed left in a
little pile for them. How can they live down here? he wondered. Yet the boys do. Once he saw a small boy try to sneak
some of the hemp seed for himself. Boris quickly thrashed
him. "*Niegadzai!*"* he cried. "The seed belongs to my bird,
you hear?"

He saw Alex watching him and swaggered over. "If you
decide to stay and learn a trade," he said, "you can learn
from watching me. I'm the best. Right now, perhaps, we are

* good-for-nothing

small potatoes, but when I am fully grown, in a few years, I shall be a really big crook. We will not just snatch things, we will rob by *kabur*.* We will be moles. It is very special work." He strolled over to his fire, holding one of the finches, which had landed to eat hemp from his fingers.

I shall really have to leave now, Alex thought, though his energy was low, and he looked wearily for the boots he had left by the fire. They were gone. They must have been kicked away, was his first thought, and he crawled about among the children on the dirt floor looking for them. His search was observed, and laughter started to spread from fire to fire, the loudest laugh coming from close by.

"Is that a boy or a scabby dog you brought us, Peter?" Boris asked in a voice that sounded as if it came from the sewers, deep and full of cracked, uneven notes. And there were the boots on the feet of his companion, Grigory, who looked more like a jackal than a boy, with his spotted face and pointed ears set high on his head. He was lying on his back, his boot-clad feet dancing in the air above him.

"All right." Alex laughed nervously. "Now I'm leaving and you may give me my boots."

"I may, may I?" Grigory tried to imitate Alex's voice. "Hear that, Boris? I may give him his boots. I may also give you a black eye and a broken nose, you snot, you *dryan*." Changing his tone, he said, "If you want something to cover your feet, help yourself from the pile of 'boots' over there," and he pointed to the rags stacked in the corners.

Alex was frightened. This was a bully far worse than any he had met in school, and there had been some. He thought he had learned how to deal with bullies: One tried not to act

---

* thieving by digging tunnels from one building to another

47

frightened, and he tried now. "As a joke, it's all right, but you can't just take away someone's things," he said reasonably. "The joke is over now, so give them back, please."

Boris said, "Hear that, comrades! The *dryan* tells us you can't take someone's things!" He now took the boots and put them on his own feet. Everyone laughed. Alex felt a wave of terror. "Tell that to the Bolsheviks!" Boris growled. "Tell them they cannot take my father's little farm, burn the fields. Yes, tell them they can't take someone's things!"

"Yes, tell them that," said Grigory, who seemed to be Boris's echo and shadow. "They burned our house and all the furniture and stole the cow and the chickens."

"Cow!" Leon said. "Don't tell me about cows! The straw tax that my father paid took the food from our cow, and she grew so weak that we had to hold her on her feet by binding strips of cloth around her and tying them to the stable roof beam. There she hung until she was so weak she died. After that, we had nothing." He blinked his pale eyelids.

Peter, who had been silent during all this, now seemed to awaken with a start. "How do you think we live?" he barked. He answered his own question. "We take what others have."

"That's how everyone lives," Kostia said.

"No," Alex said, holding hard to what he knew about life. "My father did not live that way . . . *does* not." He feared the past tense.

"Hear that, boys?" Boris chortled. "The father of the *dryan* didn't live that way. Ain't that nice!"

"And just how did this wonderful father live?" Peter asked.

"He was an educator. He worked for the state."

"And who does the state take from?" asked Boris, triumphant. "From *my* father, that's who. In fact, those may be my father's boots. So, you see, it is quite right that I have them."

"Give him back his boots," Peter now said quietly. "We do not steal from each other."

"He is not one of us. He said so himself," Boris said.

"Give them back," Peter ordered, and Boris sullenly pulled off the boots and threw them at Alex.

Where did Peter's authority come from? Alex wondered. He was not older or even as big as Boris. They were all in rags. And yet, he thought, there was something about Peter —he wore his rags differently.

Miska came and sat beside him as he put the boots on. "Read the rest of the story before you go," he said, pushing the book at him. A few of the younger boys came closer at the suggestion.

"I can't," Alex muttered. "I have to go." He went over to Peter. "Thank you," he said.

"We're even now," Peter said gruffly. "But remember, when you go out you are fair game for any of us or any of the others out there, all over Moscow, who may not be as . . . gentle as we."

"Gentle!" Alex said, looking at the filthy roughnecks in their malodorous rags, listening to their clamorous arguments and fights.

"If you think we are rough, wait until you meet with some of the others."

"I hope he does," Boris growled.

"Like Borun and his band," Kostia said, his sad, thin face looking almost pleased to be telling about it. "They'll not just steal your boots and your coat, they'll carve your liver and eat it for supper." And he laughed in a way that sounded

49

like wooden spoons hitting together, like a cough more than a laugh.

Alex turned and went toward the boarded entry. He was unsteady on his feet, strangely light-headed. Peter came and moved the boards, then led him down the dark hallway to the stairway leading to the street, going ahead and signaling when the way was clear.

"Be alert," he warned, as Alex reached the top of the stairway. "Have eyes all around your head. Good luck."

As the cold air hit Alex's lungs, an odd blinding sensation came over him. His knees became unhinged, and he fell like a rock in the snow.

He faded in and out of consciousness, sometimes feeling the heat of the fire upon him, sometimes feeling only ice, but when he had fully regained consciousness he knew he was back in the cellar. Miska was beside him, and there seemed to be only one or two other boys, one carrying water, one tending the fire.

"What happened?" Alex asked Miska, his voice strange in his ears. "I dreamed I had left this place."

"You left it, but you are back," Miska said. "I think you came back to finish the story."

Alex's mind went over his departure. It took him to the cellar door and stopped.

"You fell down," Miska said brightly, bringing him some hot water in a bowl. "There's a special herb in it. Peter said to give it to you." Alex took the bowl and drank the bitter-tasting water. Then he lay back again, feeling unable to sustain his weight. "You're sick," Miska said, "but probably you will not die. I know. I see how sickness is. Everyone is sick."

"Everyone is sick," Alex muttered. "But they are all out in the cold now."

"Of course. We have to eat. If we don't go out, we will be sicker. But there are some sicknesses that Peter will not let come to the cellar. Some very bad. He will not take those boys into the band. He will take them to the children's home if they want to go." Miska shuddered.

"And what does the children's home do with them?"

"Oh, if they have room, they give them a place on the floor to sleep, and sometimes some food if they have any. If they are going to die, they can die there." Miska seemed neither worried nor affected by these facts. "I was in one, once. Peter took me away."

Alex drifted off to sleep again. When he awoke there was the stir around him of many feet stomping in front of the rekindled fires, many voices bantering or arguing. There was coughing.

"Can't get rid of you, after all," Peter said to Alex when he saw that he was awake. "How do you feel now?"

"I feel strange—weak, hot and cold," Alex said.

"I'll give you more of our herbs for fever," Peter said, and went to a niche in the stone wall. There was a small amount of pepper, salt, vodka, napthol, cart grease, and some small twists of newspaper containing herbs. He selected one, poured boiling water over the contents, and let it steep some minutes. "Later, when you're well, you will get some herbs to replace these," he said. "That way we keep our medicine chest stocked, and whoever has a fever can have some."

Alex was too weary to ask where he was to find herbs in the middle of Moscow in winter, but he drank the brew and accepted a piece of black bread and later some cooked porridge. In the days that followed, as Alex lay on the floor of the cellar, sweating, then chilling, sleeping, and finally starting to feel better, he heard the comings and goings of the boys, and their habit of life became as familiar as his own.

He saw the tattooed names on some of their arms—Leon's was Anatole; Kostia was Vladimir. When he asked, they only said they had not always been waifs, that Leon and Kostia were the names of this life. Anatole and Vladimir were the names of that other life. He saw Ivan twirling bowls on the end of a stick, juggling stones, sometimes four in the air at once. He saw for himself why Kostia was sometimes called The Dancer—when at night, in the dim light of the waning fire, he rose from his place on the floor and moved slowly, almost gracefully about. Once Alex had started to take hold of him to guide him from the fire, but Peter had grabbed his arm. "Don't touch him," he had whispered. "He will scream and awaken everyone. Nothing happens to him." And nothing did. Alex saw, too, that Boris, who lounged about the fire whenever he was in the cellar, nevertheless slept standing up in a corner.

"He has to sleep that way," Kostia had explained. "When Boris's family was burned out of their farm, Boris was taken by a rich *kulak*° to work for him. If he ever found Boris sleeping, he would beat him. So Boris learned to sleep standing up so that he would look awake. Now he can't sleep any other way."

As for Kostia, he had left home during the famine to look for some food. "There was nothing," he said. "What little flour we had, the soldiers requisitioned." When he got to

° landed peasant

Moscow he was picked up in the great sweep that was conducted by the Commission for Social Welfare. They raided every place they could, because of the public outcry against the wild children, and threw them into children's homes. When the homes could not hold another soul, they gave up the idea. Kostia escaped. "I would rather starve in the street than starve in that sewer," Kostia said, his face twitching. "You see, we are heroes. Yes, only heroes live as we do."

One night, in the quiet of the cellar, the light of the little fires fading, the cold settling deeply, Alex, lying near Peter, whispered, "How did you find this cellar, Peter?"

"Sleep," Peter said. "Sleep is good for fevers."

"But my fever is getting better."

Almost like a parent humoring a sick child, Peter said, "All right. I'll tell you this much. I was hiding out in the city for a long time . . . longer than most of the boys in this band. My father was killed during the fighting and my mother died in the famine, always giving my baby brother and me whatever there was to eat. My aunt took us to the children's home on Ostrov Street. It was terrible then, of course, but compared to the way it is now, I suppose it would not seem so bad. There were metal bunks and a blanket, and there was usually gruel in the morning and cabbage soup at night. '*Stichi da kasha, pischa nasha*,' "* he sang in a falsetto, and laughed. "Now . . ." his voice drifted off, too.

"And then how did you get out?" Alex prompted.

"Well, when I got old enough and smart enough I would slip out for a few days at a time, get some food, and bring it back for my little brother. And then . . . then, one day I came back and he was dead. He had been beaten."

* "Cabbage soup and gruel, that's our food" (a popular ditty)

"Who beat him?" asked Alex, aghast.

"I was never sure. Perhaps the director. Perhaps one of the others."

"What did you do?" Alex tried to imagine what he would do if he found his little sister had been beaten. But he *had* found her gone . . . stolen! And what had he done? Nothing.

"Nothing," Peter said. "I did nothing. I just sat and brooded for a week, and then I went out and I stayed out forever except when they would catch me, now and then. I was hiding out all over the city, not wanting to join any bands. At first I was begging, but later, well . . . I learned the ways of the streets, the tricks. I have slept in doorways, in trees in the municipal park. I have slept in hot asphalt pots and in sewers. In freezing weather I have slept in dung heaps at the military stables. And sometimes, of course, I could get a warm piece of clothing and sell it for something to eat. That way I got to know the baker, Jacob, because anytime I got any money, I'd go and buy a little roll from him. He was the first man I had known, after my father, whom I respected and admired. He was kind, and calm, and strong, and wise. I thought I would like to be like him. I never stole from him. A lucky thing, too, because one day he said he needed someone to keep his ovens going and make deliveries to the barracks. This was me, I said, and I had the job.

"Let me tell you that to keep the bakery oven going in the winter is as good a job as you can get in the city—all the warmth you need, a roll to eat anytime you want it, a place to sleep near the fire, and a kopek after each delivery.

"But how long does anything good last! Before the winter was over they came and took the baker away. Me, I was delivering some bread to the barracks near the river. When I

54

came back the shop was locked and barred, as it was at night.

"I used to ask myself what that old man could have done to get himself in trouble. I heard someone say that he put messages in some deliveries. What messages? To whom? I never believed that.

"I was sorry that this had happened to the old man. He was the only person who had ever been good to me after my mother died. It was like having a grandfather or some such. We used to talk about many things: about living in . . . good ways, about the rights of people to choose for themselves what they will do. He had begun to teach me to read. I had learned a little. He was teaching me the bakery trade. I was really an apprentice. Then it was over."

He was silent for so long that Alex thought he had fallen asleep. "But what did you do, then? You were going to tell me about the cellar."

"Here's what I did. When I found the building all closed up, I went around to the back and slid in through the chute we used to drop wood through. I didn't dare make a fire that day, but I could curl up near the warm ashes from the oven, which the soldiers had smashed, and sleep among the empty flour sacks.

"In a few days it seemed that every building on the street was boarded up and out of business. There were no more private shops on the street. Sometimes I thought I was the only person left in the quarter. The GPU would go by in their brown vans, but that would be the only thing moving on the whole street. I didn't know what I was going to do, but I knew that the children's shelter was no warmer than the bakery cellar even without the oven.

"The GPU had taken the bags of flour, but one had broken

on the floor. I scraped some up and put it in an old mixing basin and went to the market and sold cupfuls. Then I stood in line and bought myself some sausage. I did the same thing for several days. And then one of the boys from the children's home saw me. He was standing in line at the commissary selling places like a lot of the boys do. He yelled at me and came dashing over to me after he had collected his money from the shopper. That was Boris. He came back to the cellar with me. After that, a few others from the home came with us and then other children from all over. They came and went. Sometimes we had to throw out some who would not live by our rules. I still wanted to be the kind of man Jacob, the baker, was, and we called it the Baker's Band." He paused. "Boris and I . . . we had different ideas, but it was my cellar and I was bigger than Boris then."

"Boris is bigger now," Alex said, and wondered if that had been a tactful observation.

"Yes," Peter agreed. "Boris is bigger, but bigger isn't everything. Now, shut up and sleep."

～6

The day that Alex felt almost like himself again—thinner, weaker, yet in some ways stronger—he thought, this is the day I must leave. And yet he remained another day. What held him? He did not know. Anything would be better than this, he thought—the cold, the filth, the smells, the smoke, the terrible food, the vermin. And yet, this had become something he was familiar with. He didn't know what was out there in the streets. Worse, he feared he did know.

"I'll have to go now," he said to Peter, finally.

"Okay," Peter said. "But first there's something you have to do, you know."

"What's that?" Alex asked.

"You'll have to replace the herbs we gave you for your fever. Your fever was long, and we used them all. Now, if one of us was ill, we would have none."

"But how can I do that?" Alex asked. "Nothing is growing now in the snow, and where in Moscow could they grow, anyhow?" Everyone laughed.

"Oh, *where* do they grow?" Boris mimicked. "Where *do* they grow?"

"Shut up, Boris," Peter said. "A chemist's is where they are, of course. There is still one that has not been closed in this district."

"But I have no money to buy them."

"Do you think I thought you did?" Peter said impatiently. "You'll take them, just the way we always do. Come on now, sooner is better than later."

"But I have never stolen anything," Alex protested.

"Then you'll just have to learn," Peter said, laughing. "It's a skill, a trade like any other."

"But I don't want to learn to be a thief."

Now, Peter looked angry. "Listen, fool, I've helped you until now, but you have a debt to pay. Come along. Ivan will help you. He will keep the chemist so busy in the front of the shop, you won't have any trouble at all getting the herbs from the jars in the back. And Kostia will keep watch outside. If it were not so easy, do you think I would have you do it?"

Now out into the cold they went, single file, through the cellar door and, like cellar rats, scurried against the walls, through the snowy streets and alleys, across the Moskva River to the *apteka*, the chemist's, one of the few shops still operating in a street of boarded-up buildings. Kostia posted himself outside while Alex, his heart beating fast in his chest, accompanied Ivan into the shop. Ivan started moving quickly among the displayed bottles and jars, putting his hand out as if to touch one thing, then moving to another. The chemist came from behind the heavy wooden counter, visibly worried, watching Ivan's every move.

"What do you want?" he asked, following Ivan around. "Don't touch anything."

"Comrade," Ivan said, his wide-set eyes innocent in his comical face. "Watch me carefully. I am touching nothing.

Nothing at all." He held his hands up and out in front of him, moving quickly around in the front of the store.

As instructed, Alex, with heart beating fast in his chest, eased quietly to the back of the shop and quickly ducked behind the counter where he could see the jars stacked neatly—balm, bitters, calla, camomile, celandine. . . . Quickly Alex whisked the top from a jar and dipped his hand into the dried heads of elecampane, the bitter weed that had cured his fever. A fistful in each pocket and he was out in front of the counter and ready to leave. The chemist was now red and explosive.

"This is not a place to stand," he was shouting at Ivan. "This is my shop. Out now."

"*Your* shop?" Ivan asked innocently. "I beg your pardon, comrade, I thought everything belonged to the people now. I thought this floor was mine as well as yours and that I could stand on it and enjoy the warmth and pleasant odors and admire the splendid jars, but you say no." Alex prodded him. He wanted to get out. "Very well," Ivan said sadly. "My comrade and I will leave, as you ask. Come, Sergei," he said to Alex.

"Did you get it so fast!" Ivan exclaimed when they had rejoined Kostia and were walking away quickly. Alex nodded. He was still shaking but was diverted by Ivan's dramatic performance.

"You could have been an actor," he said admiringly. "At home, I have seen traveling companies of actors, and you were just as good. Truly."

"My parents were in the circus," Ivan said proudly. "I am a circus kid. All of my brothers and sisters were. We all did a great trick together called The Mill. My father would hang upside down on the trapeze, holding a strap in his teeth.

Then slowly, to the roll of drums, he would draw each of us children up into the air on the strap, twirling, the spotlight on us, showing us wearing costumes with wings. It was magnificent."

"But why did you leave the circus?" Alex asked. "I think that would be a fine life."

"Oh, it was," Ivan said. "My father and mother were taken one night after they did a tightrope act. My father was dressed as Lenin and my mother like Trotsky, and they would teeter on the rope and then fall, every which way, into a net. People loved it. To be fair, they used to do the Czar, as well. But they were taken anyway."

They lingered along the side of the building on the square watching people come and go—peasants in their knitted hats and boots, gentlemen with canes, old grandmothers with wide peasant skirts and *babushkas*. "That was good, the way you worked in the shop," Ivan said.

Then a lady walked slowly by, carrying packages in both arms. Creeping silently behind her, Kostia, moving at the same pace, whipped out a small knife and carved a piece of fur from the back of her coat, then let her proceed, unaware of the mayhem committed upon her garment. Alex's mouth dropped open.

"I'll get sausage for dinner for that," Kostia said, waving the fur in Alex's face. They crossed the square and entered another marketplace, where Kostia dashed out of sight, returning shortly with a good-sized piece of sausage. Alex's mouth filled with anticipatory juices.

In this quarter, wherever they walked, the sharp towers and bright domes of the Kremlin could be seen. Above all, the red flag flew, but it did not mean very much to Alex. He only knew that the revolution had overthrown Czar Nicholas, but he knew there were still arguments about who was in power. His father had said Lenin was very ill.

They came into Red Square from the Iberian gate on the north. To the right, the red brick, battlemented walls of the Kremlin rose, punctuated by twenty towers. At the opposite side of the square was the many-domed cathedral of Saint Basil's, built by Czar Ivan the Terrible, a mass of color and patterns, more elaborate than anything Alex had ever seen. He remembered his uncle had told him that Czar Ivan had had the architects blinded so that they could never produce anything better. Like the other squares, Red Square was policed by soldiers, and the three boys clung to the edges as they crossed to a side street. In one corner, there was a tiny wooden booth where an old lady was selling *narzan*, water of the Caucusus. A tram clattered by, full of passengers, but carrying as well dozens of wild children who were swarming on the roofs and sides like fleas.

The three boys dodged down alleys and crossed and re-crossed the great Moskva River, which snaked through the city. Alex saw again the groups of urchins sitting on the street, sleeping or sprawling in piles on steps, running in packs like wild creatures, unkempt, filthy, rowdy. And he saw the expressions of revulsion and fear on the people's faces as the children passed.

Back at the cellar, other boys were returning from errands of their own, bringing water, clothing, rags, papers, scraps of rotting wood for the fires, stolen vegetables. Just as Alex, Ivan, and Kostia appeared, Peter arrived holding a perfect pudding. "Imagine cooling a pudding in a window unless it was meant as a gift for us!" he laughed. "Did you get the herbs?" he asked Alex.

"Yes, I got some," Alex said, emptying his pockets.

"Some! I should say you got some. That's enough for a month! You're a born thief!" he said, pounding Alex on the back.

"He was like one of us," Ivan said. "I didn't even see him go behind the counter myself."

"He's smart," Miska said. "I knew he could do it. Now he can stay with us."

The effect of this on Alex surprised him. He had planned to leave as soon as he had delivered the herbs and discharged his debt. But suddenly he found himself drawn— drawn to the warmth of Peter's compliment and Miska's confidence. Close around this little fire, he was temporarily protected from the loneliness of the dark gray-walled streets of the city by these filthy, ignorant, diseased boys who made him welcome.

"You'll stay, Alex," Miska said, pulling at his coat.

"Well, just for a little while," Alex found himself saying. He had not planned to say it. "Just until I can figure out what to do."

By then, the pudding had been divided into many tiny pieces. There wasn't more than a taste for each, but the experience was nourishing to the spirit.

"If you stay," Peter said, "you must work. Everyone here must work to eat. And you must follow our rules or we will throw you out."

"What are the rules?" Alex asked, looking at this hodge-podge of a kennel, thinking of this disordered, helter-skelter existence.

"No drinking," said Boris sullenly.

"*He* doesn't like that," Miska hissed to Alex.

Alex laughed. "But I don't drink alcohol," he said. "I

would not be allowed, except for water with a little wine in it. Where would you get wine or vodka, anyway?"

Grigory poked Miska. "I thought you said that one was smart," he growled.

"You wouldn't ask if you had been taken in by some of the other bands," Ivan said. "That is what they do with most of the money they steal: They buy vodka."

"Or cocaine," Basil said.

"And no cocaine here, or other such thing," Peter said. "Just once and we throw you out by the seat of your pants."

"You must not bring any boys here who have typhus or syphilis," Peter continued.

Alex could hardly believe these rules. He had thought they'd be something like school rules—something to do with duties, perhaps, punishments for failure to do one's share.

"These are some of the important everyday rules," Peter said. "Our band is different from most other bands. This is Jacob the Baker's Band. We are here because of him."

"But how many bands are there?" Alex asked.

"Who can tell!" Kostia answered. "Hundreds. When we go south, you will see it is like a river of boys." He laughed. "Last year, they tried to keep us all out of Tashkent just to save the melons from us locusts."

"I can't wait to go for the melons," said Miska, swallowing saliva as he thought of the juicy fruit.

"You made yourself sick with melons," Kostia said.

"So did you," Miska replied. "Everyone does. When can we go, Peter?"

"In spring, as usual, stupid. If we went now, we would be eating green fruits, and everyone knows there is not as good a living, otherwise, in the south. Peasants have no pockets."

Everyone laughed. "There is little to steal and nobody has any money to buy it," Kostia said. "They have food growing in the fields, but when that is not growing, there is nothing else for us."

"There is one more rule and it is the most important," Peter said. "We do not kill."

"Kill!" Alex cried.

"Listen," Peter said almost angrily, "there are many, many homeless ones in this city and all the cities and towns. They all need what we need—something to eat, somewhere to sleep and keep warm. They must try to get it as they know how. We try to get it with our skills. Others, without skills, do it with their fists, rocks, sticks, knives. If you are in danger, perhaps you may have to protect yourself, but you must not kill if you are with us. It is not their fault that they have something we need, any more than it is our fault that we need it. And for the people who do not like our rules"—Peter glanced around the smoky cellar meaningfully, accusingly—"for those people, there are other bands who will have them."

Miska now came up with his old red book. He said nothing, just pressed it upon Alex. Once again, Alex opened the volume and read of the spirits that lived in folklore: of the *vodyanoi*, who haunted the waters, bearded and ugly. It was he who caused the storms at sea, who smashed ships, caused floods. On the other hand, when he was feeling pleasant, he would lead the fish into the fishermen's nets. In the waters with him lived the beautiful *rusaiki*, who sang so beautifully in the moonlight that some of the fishermen would drown themselves seeking them.

64

Miska listened, as did some of the others, and their faces were tense and anxious as were all Russian children's when they heard of these ancient spirits. But how, Alex wondered, would these children fear such spirits, when they did not fear running homeless and starving on the streets of Moscow?

"Today," Peter said to Alex, "you will go with Kostia and Ivan again. They are good knockers. They will show you how a knocker works. It is a good way for you to begin. All you will do is stand guard, just the way you did when you helped Miska."

"I wasn't standing guard. I was just there."

"That's it. You will just be there and you will keep your collar up around your face so that you can do it over and over and no one will recognize you. Be careful. Remember, if you are caught, we are all in danger."

Alex followed Kostia and Ivan out of the cellar. They were both smaller than he, their faces almost black with the oily smoke of the fire, their scrawny bodies covered in the same dreadful rags they all wore. Beside them Alex felt handsomely clad, although his coat was now torn and covered with soot and oily stains. His boots could hardly be seen beneath the encrusted dirt. They moved swiftly, holding close to the gray walls of the building until they came out on a street near a market Alex had not seen before. They waited as a procession of workers marched by, bearing flags and signs against capitalism. Just as they were entering the square, a tall woman in a black coat and heavy black boots passed them. She wore her hair in a low knot held in place by a decorative tortoise comb. Quicker than a darting bug in a pond, Ivan's hand shot up and claimed the comb. Alex's breath caught in his throat. Would the woman scream? She did not. She kept on walking, never having felt the swift hand that took her comb. Now, incredibly to Alex, Ivan approached the woman, running along beside her.

"Madame!" he called. "I would like to sell you a handsome comb for your hair." The woman ignored him, but he persisted, dancing in front of her and waving the comb. "Twenty kopeks only, madame, for this beautiful work of art." The woman stopped.

"But that's just like mine," she cried, touching her hair. "It *is* mine, you little thief! Give it back this instant."

Ivan looked shocked. "No, no. You are mistaken. This is mine, but I will offer it to you, since you have none, for only fifteen kopeks. Now that's a bargain you'll not find again. You would have to pay four times that to buy a new one."

The woman sighed. She knew it was true. "Filty little robber," she muttered, and put some coins in his hand. Ivan bowed and handed her the comb.

"Why did Peter want me to come along for that?" Alex asked. "I didn't do anything, and I would never be able to do anything like that myself. You must have a touch like feathers."

"Oh, that wasn't the place you were to stand guard," Kostia said. "That was a little extra Ivan did on the spur of the moment. We have to take opportunity where we find it. Okay, now," he continued, "I am going to duck into the alley just there. You will lean here against the building. Walk back and forth a little now and then and look at the sky. Pretend you are waiting for someone. If a soldier is in sight, you are supposed to start whistling. Can you whistle?" he asked anxiously.

"Yes, but what about Ivan?"

"You just do your job. He will do his."

Alex leaned against the building. A wet wind blew around and out of the square. He pulled his collar up and remembered that Peter had said to keep his face hidden. He pulled his cap down. Meanwhile Ivan seemed to be doing the same thing a little farther down the street. He looked much like a person waiting for someone who is late, looking around impatiently. He would leave his place a minute, start off somewhere, and then return. A few people passed and paid no attention to him or to Kostia. A dumpy peasant woman, layered in scarves and skirts, went by carrying a roll of rags on her shoulder. An old man passed, ill-dressed, limping, pulling a heavy package in the snow. Then a stout woman appeared at the corner. She wore a warm wool coat and carried a large, heavy handbag. Kostia seemed not to notice her, but, as she came abreast of him, he suddenly fell and sprawled on the ground directly at her feet, causing her to lose her balance, teeter, and fall. Alex was alarmed. Had the same thing that had happened to him happened to Kostia—a fever, perhaps? He started to run toward him but stopped when he saw Ivan spring out of the alley, grab the woman's handbag, and disappear back down the alley with Kostia, suddenly revived, right behind him. Alex had the impulse to help her—she seemed so distressed—but something pulled him away, and he turned quickly and followed Kostia and Ivan, who were waiting for him at the end of the alley. They grabbed him and pulled him under a wall and into an empty lot. There, behind a pile of trash, Kostia ripped open the bag. A scent of perfume arose from it that bit into Alex's memory for a moment and made him close his eyes. Kostia was digging like a rabbit making a burrow. He produced two rubles and a handkerchief. He put the handkerchief in his pocket and the bag under his jacket, making him only a little lumpier than he was anyway.

Now they skirted the early-morning streets, crossed the Moskvoretsky Bridge to another market, more organized and crowded than those they had visited before. As they went, Alex kept noting the wild flights of the ragged children, sometimes shrieking like pack-wolves, sometimes silent. Then other times they appeared to be dried leaves blowing before a strong wind, circling. Here and there small children begged and were occasionally given a coin and young girls holding up infants cried, "A kopek to feed my baby, only a kopek."

Now they were in Sverdloff Square, its garden filled with snow where Alex had remembered a mosaic of geraniums and begonias when he visited his uncle. The great opera house dominated the square, and at the curb were the old carriage drivers, the *izvotschiks*, wearing heavy patched cloaks and fur bonnets, looking like great sleeping bears as they waited for their fares. Do people really travel in these anymore? Alex wondered. The *izvotschiks* seemed left there from some grander, quieter time. Also left from a grander day was a statue of a chariot and horses in the middle of the square, now swathed in scaffolding.

They turned into a street where a line of people stretched in a snake around a corner. Into this line, Ivan pushed Alex. "You stand here," he said.

"But why?" Alex asked.

"Because, blockhead, at the end of the line is bread. That is the government store. I'll be back before you reach the end. Dance about and your feet won't freeze in place. Kostia will be close by."

With that, Ivan disappeared, but Kostia slowly walked in and out of the line of people, peddling the handbag. Alex worried that Kostia would be arrested, but the people in the line seemed unsurprised to be approached by a thief. Those Alex saw merely shook their heads and seemed to pin their attention on the slow progress of the line. He waited nervously, standing on one frozen foot and then the other, and, as he waited, a well-dressed man came up and pressed a kopek into his hand, saying, "Hold a place for me, boy," and quickly left. In a short time, a woman came and did the same. By the time Kostia reappeared, cheerfully holding up two rubles, Alex had collected coins from four customers who returned and took their places in front of him.

So now, he said to himself, I am like the urchin to whom Katriana Sergyeva gave a kopek that day so long ago. In the excitement of this morning's lessons in thievery in the square, in the days spent in the cellar, it had not been nearly so clear as this. I am just such a waif as they, he said to himself, and again the terrible feeling of loss took hold.

"Alex! You dumb ox!" Ivan was shaking him. "You have to keep moving about or you'll freeze standing in one place. Here, it is nearly our turn. Ask for two loaves," and he pushed a coin into Alex's hand.

They each got the maximum, two loaves, and, tucking them under their arms, returned the way they had come, crossing the snowy city. The snow clung in great globules around the wire cages on the street lamps, which the government installed to keep them from being stolen. The boys threw balls of snow at them to make them fall in explosive bursts.

Everywhere the bands of wild children moved through the snow or appeared suddenly from under an abandoned wagon, an old packing case. They huddled among the trash and ashes of the back alleys. They flew like wounded birds against the new snow.

The aroma of the bread tortured them all the way, yet none took a bite. Alex already knew from his days in the cellar that all the food was the property of everyone in the band and that it must be divided by the person in charge that day. Peter, just coming in from an errand of his own, met them and praised their contribution to the day's meal. Leon took the bread and cut it carefully with the short, sharp blade that was kept in the wall. What doesn't that wall contain? Alex wondered. Kostia threw a good-sized sausage onto the low, makeshift table made of a board balanced on stones. Kostia emptied his pockets of a handful of groats.

"Some good morning's work!" Peter said as the children came around for their portions. The groats were thrown into a kettle of water, and by the time their feet had begun to thaw a bit, a bowl of thin, hot gruel was ready to eat.

"When did you get those groats?" Alex asked Kostia.

"Hand fast; eye slow," he said.

"We'll keep the sausage for tonight," Peter said. "Two meals are better than one."

"It's a good day when we have two meals," Kostia said.

From the next fire, a voice growled, "It's a good day when we have one."

In the silences of the cellar, the children moved in a world of their own. No sounds of Moscow reached them here, no sights. In the cellar, no GPU, no soldiers, no hard-faced officials tried to catch them and detain them in children's homes no better than a jail.

"Here, at least, if we are hungry, cold, and filthy, we are those things while we are free," Peter had said. "We are alive

70

and we are free," he had said at another time when they were bitterly cold and the food was scarce. "This is more than many people are."

In the smoke and blankness of the cellar crypt, it was possible to imagine a world in which everyone was warm, everyone was fed, everyone lived under the protection of a family. As he lay on the dirt floor in his fetid clothes, scratching where the fleas and lice were attacking, feeling his only-partly-filled belly, Alex pretended that this was not a country at war with itself. He imagined things as they were so long ago when he might be walking out in the winter sun with his family, nodding at neighbors, not running through the city's streets like one of the rats. Alex pretended that order and love were still alive and that he was only camping with old Tolka in the forest near Kovrov, that he had dug through the snow to the fallen leaves, as Tolka had shown him, and made a warm bed under the snow, and in the morning . . . in the morning, he would be going home.

All over Moscow, in other cities, in towns, and on the roads, children slept . . . and not safely in their beds. They slept in doorways, in cellars, in empty ruins. They slept like lumps of charcoal in the middle of Moscow streets, in asphalt cauldrons in which the fires had died. Hundreds and thousands of the homeless slept, deserted, except by each other.

71

~7

Day after day—and Alex lost count—he joined the boys in scouting the cold city in the early morning and at dusk, scraping at its ribs for food, fighting the cold, the wind, the snow, avoiding the soldiers and the police. Alex had become adept at identifying the arms of the law—the regular police in their black uniforms, red caps, carrying revolvers and clubs; the GPU in khaki with green caps; and the soldiers who carried rifles with fixed bayonets.

As time went by, Alex came to blend with the urchins. Even his fine coat and boots were so shabby and wet they were not salable anymore. Nevertheless, they embarrassed him, and he felt resentment from some of the boys when he pried his cold feet into his wet boots, while they rewrapped theirs in grimy rags.

But the younger boys were so respectful of his ability to read that with them Alex felt quite dignified—almost like his father. He read to them from Miska's book of folktales about *vedemy*, dreadful old witches who lived in a hovel that moved on chicken's feet. But also Alex became an educator. He began to try to teach a few of the most eager boys to read. Once he brought back to the cellar a handbill from a fence and used its big letters to instruct them.

"This is an A. Here is an F and a G." And he would hunt for the alphabet in the sign. "Do you see these words? They say 'Do Not.' Now, when you see those words on a sign, you will know what they say. You can *read* them." The boys were entranced that they could read the two words.

Sometimes, during these lessons, Peter lingered around the edge of the circle, wrapping his feet, whittling with his knife, or just lying nearby with eyes slightly open. Alex never asked him or anyone to join the circle, though he would have liked to. He was more educated, but he did not feel Peter's equal here in the streets of Moscow.

It was cold when Alex had arrived in Moscow and it had never ceased to be so, but now it was more bitter than ever. Boris's finches had died, leaving him angry. He stamped around in the cellar, his breath steaming in front of him, and Alex had the feeling it was his anger that he was venting.

On a cold January day, Alex and Ivan stood in a long line, despite the cold, collecting money for holding places. Food was getting scarce again, and the vendors in the market were not standing out in the cold with their meager vegetables. One needed kopeks to buy the government bread. Beside the line, several old women sold tea made from hot water from portable samovars. The people in the line stood silent in the long, long snaking curve. The snow fell silently above them. The building was draped in red flags with black borders.

"Come on," Ivan said, when their clients had returned to claim their places. "Let's get back in the line again."

"No, wait," Alex said. "As long as we're here, let's see him."

"Why do you want to see a dead man?" Ivan said.

Alex didn't know, but in a few minutes he was looking down into the face of Lenin, the head of the government, who had died a few days before. Once, when he was very, very young, Alex's father had taken him to see the Czar ride by in a carriage. He didn't know if he really remembered it or if he remembered his father telling him of it. What would his father say if he knew that he had stood and looked into the dead face of one of the people who had overthrown the Czar's government?

The weather blocked Moscow from food from the outside. The government bread stores opened infrequently. The vendors and peddlers had disappeared. Kostia and Alex were standing in the square, in the shelter of a building. Swarms of other children drifted by like passing storms, their tight little faces red with cold, their eyes dark with circles, limbs flailing to combat the wind. And from one such flight, a small girl, struggling to keep up, stumbled and fell into snow too deep for her. She lay there, abandoned in the marketplace, as her flock flew on without her. Alex expected the girl to get up and run to join her companions, but she did not. She lay in the snow, her tears freezing on her face. It was then that Alex's feet took him out to the middle of the square.

"Leave her!" Kostia hissed, but, for perhaps for the first time, Alex paid no attention to the orders of others. The wind blew snow around in a way that would soon cover the child, but she did not move to help herself. Alex bent down.

"Get up!" he said sternly. "You will freeze." He reached his hand out to help her. She seemed very small, very pale, from what one could see beneath the smears of dirt and the patches of snow. "Come," Alex said, and he half pulled her across the square to the wall against which the children were huddled.

"You should have left her," Kostia said. "The soldiers

74

would have found her. Now what are you going to do with her?"

"Take her back to the cellar, of course. What else can we do?"

"We don't have girls," Ivan said. "They're too much trouble. Everyone knows that. And this one is too small."

"Miska is small," Alex said.

"But Miska is smart and he is not half dead, and besides, he is a boy and can keep up with us," Kostia replied.

"Miska was half dead when Peter found him in the children's home in the south, Ivan told me." He gave the little girl a tap as if he might burn his hand. "What's your name?"

"Anya," the child said, her eyes wide, looking with fright at her judges. She shivered uncontrollably, and Alex took off his heavy coat and threw it over her. It trailed around her comically.

"Come, we'll take her over to the children's home on Potchtovaia Street and leave her at the gate," Kostia said. The child turned to run and would have had she not been mired in snow that continued to fall.

"No!" she screamed.

"But they will take care of you and feed you," Alex said.

The child gave him a look that would have burned a hole in a good pot and then uttered an obscenity that stunned him, coming from that small mouth. He tried to imagine his little sister uttering such an oath, and his mind would not permit it. "I was there," Anya said. "My brother and I ran away. I would never go back. Not ever."

"Where is your brother, then?" Alex asked.

"The soldiers got him. They said he was too old to be a *bezprizoni*. They put him in prison. I don't know where he is."

"How old was he?" Kostia asked.

"About fifteen, but he was very big and strong." Now she started to cry again.

"We can't stand here all day talking about it," Kostia said. "You take her back to the cellar and let Peter settle it. I've got better things to do. I'm going to try the other market and see if there's anything stirring." He was off like an animal in the snow, foraging.

Alex led the frozen child down the streets and back to the now familiar cellar that he had begun to regard as his home. Strange how the dank and odorous place radiated welcome when compared with the heavy skies and emptiness of the city streets.

Miska was tending the fire and, when Alex entered, ran to meet him. "What have you got? We have water nearly boiling," he called.

"We found nothing," Alex said. "There is no food coming into the city."

"Peter will find some," Miska said. "Peter almost always finds some. Who is that boy?"

"That boy is a girl," Alex said, laughing. "Her name is Anya. She fell in the snow and was left by her band. Will you look out for her until I come back?"

"A girl!" Miska said. "Well, come to the fire and get warm." Alex left them.

In a few hours everyone was back empty-handed except for Kostia, who had the kopeks from selling a coat he had stolen but said he could not buy bread for them. Peter came in panting. "That was close," he said. "Too close. I took the lunch pails of four soldiers from the barracks. They chased me clear around Moscow. Wouldn't you think the *sooksins* would have something better to do?" The pails yielded a small amount of bread and some cold boiled potatoes. It was not much for so many hungry children, but it was something. When Boris complained about the size of his portion, Peter laughed harshly. "It's more than those four soldiers are having!"

Now for the first time, in the dim light, he caught sight of Anya, who had been asleep in a corner. "Who is that one?" Alex thought it was the first time he had seen Peter show surprise. He always seemed to accept everything as it happened.

Alex said, "Her name is Anya. She's been abandoned by her band. We found her in the snow. Please let her stay, Peter."

"We have no room for girls," Peter said, turning away.

"Please, Peter. We can't throw her out in the snow."

"That's where you found her, isn't it? Stand up," he ordered Anya. "Look how small she is. Who is to look after her when we are on the move? Tell me that!"

"I will," Alex said. "I have looked after my little sister at home."

"And I will," Miska piped. "And she doesn't take much food."

"Has anyone kept anything to eat from their ration?" Peter asked. "She should have something now." Alex had seen Boris and some of the boys put small bits of food in their shirts from time to time. He wished he could learn to squirrel away some of his ration himself, but he was always too hungry. Now, it was only Ivan who came forth.

Alex looked around at the boys he could see in the firelight. Finally Leon said, "All right. Here's a bit more." He reached under his shirt. Miska brought a bowl of hot water.

"No one has to look after me," Anya said, after she had gobbled up the food in a few bites. "I look after myself. I even tie my own boots. Look!" She held up her tiny feet wrapped in rags.

"Here," Peter said. "We will give you new boots." He showed her where the pile of rags was. "We'll decide what to do with you later."

In the night a fierce wind blew the snow in drifts against the entrance to the cellar. When they had cleared a way to the street, it was to find that icy winds still blew, gnawing at their ill-covered bodies, and they had to move quickly to keep from freezing to the spot. Once again, the marketplace was a snowy field. There would be no peddlers today. They retreated to the relative warmth of the cellar. Only Peter stayed out in the bitter weather. When he returned it was empty-handed and with bad news. "Almost nothing is coming into the city," he said. "The farmers have used up all their winter stores of potatoes, cabbages, and grains, and any carts coming toward the city have been raided by hoodlums." He looked around at the band of children, huddled around the smoking fires, taking what little warmth could be had from them. "We must make plans," he said. "It is much too early, but I think we will have to go south. It will be less cold than here, and there must be something in the fields—roots, at least."

"And melons!" shouted Miska.

"No melons yet, dumbhead," Leon said.

"We'll go down to the station at dawn and wait for the first train south," Peter said. "Let's build up the fires with all the trash now, because we will not be this warm for a while."

It was possible in the firelight to kindle hope of a promised land, to push aside anxiety, the cold, the damp, the irritation of lice and fleas, the pain of separation, loss, loneliness.

~8

They were at the Kazan Station before it was fully light, their breath steaming a way for them through the frosty air. There was nothing moving. A few early passengers were stamping about, waiting for the train south, but their stamping was muffled by the snow. In the corners were the same kind of dirty, living sacks Alex had seen at the station at Kovrov. When Leon approached one of the passengers, begging, he was immediately knocked into the snow by one of the sacks that had leapt up. "You can't work here, you *svolotch*. This is our territory." The passenger backed off nervously, leaving the two urchins to battle it out.

"You don't own the station," Leon protested.

"We own the right to work in this station," the boy snarled, "and if you want us to prove it, we will."

Peter came up. "Go back to your band," he said. "We have not come to work. We are just waiting to leave." To Leon he said, "Don't you have more sense than to call attention to us now?" He was angry.

"But Peter, this station doesn't belong to them."

"Maybe it does, in a way. The cellar belongs to us, doesn't it? They are here working it and so they are protecting their working place. Do you want to fight over that and get us all picked up?"

In a short time the station was teeming with people dressed in woolens and furs, the vapor rising from their mouths mixed with the steam of the engine of the train for the Caucusus. The enormous portraits of Lenin and Marx looked sternly down upon the platform where dozens of children, wrapped in rags, plied their trade—begging, stealing—while others leaned against the walls of the station smoking, laughing, poking fun at the behavior of the travelers.

But not all the travelers were well-dressed. Peasants and working people carrying bundles of their possessions crowded into the less-comfortable carriages, arranging themselves on wooden benches. In the corner a poorly-dressed man took a piece of bread from his pocket and sat down to eat it. Immediately, he was surrounded by ten children who watched his mouth open and close on each bite, their eyes stealing the bread from him, poisoning it. He took two more bites, hesitating before each one, then broke the rest in bits and handed it to them. "Take it. Go on. Eat it all!" and he boarded the train, angrily.

"All passengers board!" the train guard called when the *tretyzvonok* rang, and the steam swirled up in great clouds from the engine. Alex's heart beat fast as he followed Peter and the rest of the band along the gray walls of the station and across the tracks to the side of the train away from the platform.

"Where are we going to sit?" he asked Kostia, who was next to him.

"We have reserved seats," Kostia laughed, in his hard, mirthless way. Peter pointed and gave Ivan and Leon a shove. They dove under the train and, to Alex's horror, climbed into a small black box slung beneath the carriage.

"Not in *there!*" he whispered to Kostia.

"Where else, your highness? In the first-class carriages, perhaps?" Peter pointed to the black box beneath the next carriage. "There, you two."

"What about Anya?" Alex asked.

"I shall see to her myself," Peter said. "We don't want anyone falling onto the tracks."

"But this isn't big enough for a dog," Alex protested.

"Oh, yes it is," Kostia said. "That's just what it's for. Only not many dogs are traveling these days, so we can have their berths. I wish you were a dog, in fact, because then I could eat you."

"You wouldn't," Alex said, disgusted.

"Wouldn't I?"

"Have you ever, really?"

"Are you fooling? Certainly. Everyone has. So have you. I brought some myself to the cellar, one day when you were ill. Why do you look like that? Would you prefer human meat?"

Alex thought he might vomit. He thought of his dog, Sergei, at home. When he had disappeared, had it been because someone had eaten him? "Kostia," he said, "you make too many jokes like that. You say things like . . . like people eating people. You say it a lot." Kostia said nothing. A terrible thought came to Alex, but he dismissed it. "Well, I know you've never done *that*, Kostia. Kostia? *Have* you?" He whispered that, and yet he knew the answer would be negative. Still, he needed Kostia to confirm it, to say he was joking as he always joked in his hard, unsmiling way.

"Yes," Kostia answered, and he said it quietly, without the animation of his usual conversation. "But we did not kill anyone," he hurried to add. "It was sold to us. We would have starved in the villages that time, otherwise. I did not know who it was."

Alex was numb from cold and from horror. "How did you feel?" he whispered, and his whisper hissed into the steam of the engine as the train slowly began to move.

After a bit, Kostia answered, "I was glad it was not me."

The train picked up steam, and the biting cold of the wind chilled the black boxes of children packed like fish, salted with soot and grime, trundling their way to a dream world of warmth and food. Cold, hunger, anxiety, and fatigue, added to the motion of the train, finally dragged Alex into sleep, and he had no idea how much time had passed when he awoke, startled. The train was standing still, and his limbs and back felt as if they had been struck with a cleaver. A guard was shouting, "Out of there, wretches, or I will beat you to pulp with this club," and he poked into the boxes, prodding the children, who leapt out and dashed from under the train.

"Where are we?" Alex asked Kostia.

"I don't know. Maybe Lipersk. Maybe Voronezh. It's all the same until we are in the south. Cold. Come on, we may be able to get something to eat," and he led Alex back under the train. In the station they saw the better-dressed people descending to get tea and food. Old grannies, swathed in woolens and scarves, carrying buckets on yokes, stood about selling water for a kopek a glass. Alex caught sight of Miska and some of the other boys. Ivan was carrying Anya and extending his hat to some of the travelers.

"My sister is very ill," he said. "I must get her some hot tea." Anya hung in his arms so limply that Alex was alarmed.

A gentleman dropped a coin into the hat, and Ivan was off to the tea peddler with Anya, marvelously recovered, hurrying behind him.

Kostia said, "Come on, let's get some tea and some bread."

"But we have no money."

"We do now," Kostia said, holding up a few kopeks.

"Where did you get them?"

"The hand is fast; the . . ."

". . . eye is slow," Alex laughed. "I remember."

"Watch everything," a lady said to her family. "Those dreadful children are everywhere like a plague."

"Here is a piece of stale bread," a man said to his son. "You may give it to them if you wish."

"Oh, yes," said the child. "Let's see which one I will give it to. No, not that one, or that one . . ."

And then they were boarding again. This time all the black boxes seemed to fill up before Kostia and Alex got to them. "Well, it's the pipe under the engine then, if we hurry and if we're lucky," Kostia said, and quickly led Alex to the front of the train, just about to leave. Alex could not believe that he was following Kostia into a sooty pipe, barely big enough around to accommodate their bodies. "This is a little warm, at least," Kostia said. "That's the good in it." That was the only good in it. Alex could scarcely breathe for the soot lodged in the pipe, nor move for the tiny diameter of the space into which they were wedged. He did not know how much time passed this way. It seemed interminable, he was so cramped and uncomfortable.

But somewhere in the journey a miracle happened, and Alex saw it as time rolling back to a better day. The snow became less dense, then mixed with patches of brownish-yellow earth, then almost disappeared. There appeared after many hours a thin veil of tannish-green upon the ground that flew by them. The fields. The bitter cold moderated, and the chilly air seemed balmy compared to Moscow's deep cold. When Kostia and Alex poked their heads out of the pipe, they were traveling slowly through countryside with virtually no snow, except on distant mountains. Green showed on some low bushes and on trees in the distance, although all those around the cities had been felled for fuel. The sight caused Kostia to shout loudly like a horse that had been frightened by a bear. Alex's line of vision beneath the carriages permitted him a view of other children peeking out of black boxes, seeing a world that was not wholly bleak, chilled, hopeless.

The noise of the engine did not permit conversation, even freedom of motion to bang Kostia on the back, as he wished. For the first time in the months since he left his home, Alex felt joy. Immediately guilt struck him. How can I laugh and feel happy? he thought. He would not have believed, if someone had told him, that it was, indeed, possible to feel joy and pain at the same time.

～9

The train slowed and stopped, and from atop the carriages, from the boxes under them, jumped, rolled, crawled scores of children, ignoring the shouting guards, laughing at them and at the regular passengers who regarded their blackened faces and sooty rags with disgust and fear. Ivan and Kostia sat on the embankment and started to peel off one layer of rags, taking with it some of the soot and leaving a slightly less filthy layer beneath. Alex removed his jacket and shook it out. Soot rose from it as from the engine.

"Where's Anya?" Alex asked anxiously. Though he had volunteered her care, they all seemed to share it without question. She was seen close by picking pale greenish-yellow shoots and arranging them in a nosegay, stuffing every other one into her mouth.

"Will we go to the hills," Ivan asked Peter, "or stay near the river?"

"I think we will go to the caves," Peter said. "It is so early in the year, probably not too many others have come yet."

"Usually, Peter won't let us stay with the other bands in the caves because of their sicknesses and . . . and other things," Kostia said. "But I stayed in the caves once, before I met Peter. There were hundreds of children in our cave. The bosses are older boys—too old for the bands, really—and you give part of everything to them . . . *most* of everything."

"Part of what? What you find every day?" Alex asked.

"Yes, that, too, but they taught us the mountain trails, and we smuggled all kinds of things for the big bosses—men from the towns. There are thousands of children up here in the summer—thousands and thousands. They own the mountains."

Somehow the children of the various bands reformed into their own groups and took off in various directions, running along the roads, shedding rags like feathers on the way.

"First, we eat," Peter said. "Then we will find a place to stay."

"Let's go to the market then," Boris said.

"No," Peter said. "It will be slow work to get enough down there. We will have to go out to the fields."

"But it's early," Boris complained. "There will be nothing to see. We will have to dig."

"That won't hurt you," Kostia said. "Peter's right. We could cut out a hundred pockets there and not find enough for bread."

"If there's bread to buy," Peter said.

So they took off over the interlaced fences into the fields, still hard from the winter frosts, giving up the odor of earth that Alex had almost forgotten. Now it reached his senses with such an impact that they were confused and communicated that this was something to eat. He salivated. Anya picked up some of the soil and chewed it. Her little face, full of soot, now became frosted with mud.

When Alex said, "Ugh," she was unabashed.

"This is very good earth," she said. "There are even some good worms." Alex gagged.

The fields stretched before them now, row upon furrowed row, with faint touches of green in some places. They raced to these spots and began to pick the green tops of unknown plants, eating them ravenously. "Be careful," Peter warned. "Your belly can ache a lot from that. It is better to dig the roots."

"My belly aches so much now, a little more won't matter," Ivan said.

"Here, this looks right," Peter said, and began to dig with his hands and the tip of a little stick. "This is what we want," and he pulled from the ground a small tuber, the awakening roots of this year's crop of potatoes. One by one, the children abandoned the greens and turned into burrowing animals, down on their hands and knees, throwing the dirt behind them, discovering, devouring the roots.

Before they had eaten their fill, a man on a limping horse came shouting toward them, waving a whip and urging barking dogs to attack. "Urchins, scavengers, destroyers of crops. Away! Away!"

The children flew across the fields, jumped down into a trench separating the field from the roads, and ran a distance, doubled over to hide themselves from the angry *kulak*. They lay in the trench laughing and munching the last of the roots until he had disappeared, howling curses to the empty field.

Although the wind blew cold, the absence of snow was a gift, and Alex felt almost comfortable, almost hopeful. Now, he thought, although they would have to scrounge more for food and perhaps could not eat much more of these greens, they were better off than in Moscow where they were freezing and would soon have starved. Well, then, they would stay here in the south and warm themselves up and feed their empty bellies, and then . . . and then. Alex found a blank when he tried to think ahead. There seemed only to be the present. Between now and the future there hung a great dark curtain that he could not see through or around. He allowed himself to imagine going back home to Kovrov and finding his mother, father, sister, and grandmother waiting for him. "Where have you been, Alex? We missed you. Sit down to supper." And they would bring out boiled meat surrounded with vegetables in rich gravy. And a sweet cake filled with preserves. Could that be the future?

They started the climb up the rocky hill where once flocks had roamed. "They don't dare pasture the sheep and goats anymore," Boris said. "They know we'd take them all. How would you like a nice roast leg of young spring lamb, now, eh?"

"Not me," Miska said in a mournful voice. "I'm not hungry." Everyone laughed.

Alex was surprised by the cave. It was so big. He had thought of the kind of little cave he found when in the woods with old Tolka. Peter told them to stay well back of him. He entered by himself and approached a boy near the first fire. "Which one is the chief?" he asked.

"Who are you to ask?" the boy said, looking up, sleepy-eyed, dragging his head back and looking through slitted eyes. Alex knew this kind of face. Boris had this look. These people came from Mongolia. They had an Oriental cast to their features, just one of many groups of Russians. It made them look slow, but they were not.

"I'm Peter. I'm the head of this band. We have just come from Moscow and we want to stay here tonight. Tomorrow we will look for our own shelter."

The boy grunted. He was chewing a piece of a strange flat bread that Alex had not seen before.

"There's still room," the slit-eyed boy said. "But we have first rights to everything. You will have to wait your turn."

"Rights to what?" Alex whispered.

"Water, for one thing," Ivan said. "There's a stream." He pointed, and Alex could see many boys and a few girls lined up with bowls and small tins.

"Peter won't let us drink it without boiling, anyway," Kostia said, "because they foul it and many of them are sick."

Peter herded the group into a corner away from the others who seemed to hang like bats from the walls or basked in front of smoky fires.

Resting now, Alex watched the other bands. For the most part, they were a surly bunch, but, he thought, we are no group of gentlemen ourselves. Many fights were going on. Some were picking fleas from one another. Some were sharpening little homemade knives on stones. Many were scabby, some twisted and swollen. "Stay away from them," Peter warned. But despite the warning, Alex noticed Boris and Grigory in conversation with the Mongolian boy. Sleep came, in this strange place, as naturally as in any other.

In the morning, Boris was gone. So was Grigory, but they arrived back while the rest of the band was preparing to leave.

"Where have you been?" Peter asked. "We almost left without you."

"What business is it of yours?" Boris asked, even more surly than usual.

"You know what business it is of mine," Peter said.

"Where were you?" Alex thought he saw Boris exchange warning looks with the Mongolian. Did he imagine it?

"I was getting water."

"Where's the water?" Peter challenged.

"I drank it."

"You know we boil water, here."

"That's your business, too?" Boris said.

"Why is Peter grilling him like that?" Alex asked Kostia.

"Because those boys are in the drug traffic," Kostia answered. "Peter doesn't betray them, but he won't let his band work for them."

A boy from one of the other bands had just brought a basin of water to the Mongolian and was now wrapping his feet in rags for him.

"Look at that *svolotch*," Ivan whispered. "He's got himself a slave."

"He probably won him playing cards," Kostia said matter-of-factly.

Miska's belly was giving him terrible pain. "It's like last year," Peter said. "You eat too much. You will have to stay here while we go into the town." Miska whimpered and doubled up on his side.

They followed Peter down the hill past peasant cottages and little farms. As they approached the town, Alex could see through open doorways and mica windows of the cottages. They were furnished with only simple benches, a table, a stove. Goatskins hung from nails, dried sunflowers from the rafters. In one, a *muzik* slept on the stove. But this was the first time since leaving Kovrov that Alex had been in a homely town, and he felt a deep longing.

It was surprising to see the town so crowded. Alex had expected a small-town emptiness, but the streets were thronged with poor people in colorful costumes, the men long-bearded, the women wearing striped aprons, heavy skirts, and *babushkas*. Many urchins thronged the streets, begging. Open trucks of soldiers passed frequently. *Stranik*, wandering holy men, in long robes, prayed and asked for alms.

Alex was walking beside Ivan. "This is where I open my shop," Ivan said. Alex laughed. But then as he watched, Ivan spread a rag upon the ground and in it dropped two kopeks. Then he put his head down between his feet, and suddenly his feet shot into the air and he was standing on his head. Then he started to hum a bright tune. Now Alex was laughing so hard he couldn't stop. It felt good. Several passers-by stopped and looked at Ivan. Now he started rotating, pushing himself around with his hands, nearly spinning on his head. Then he lowered his legs, forward, then backward, then one forward and one back. Then, with a push, he propelled himself to his feet. The people clapped and smiled. Ivan bowed deeply. A man threw a kopek onto the rag.

"See," Ivan complained. "That's the south for you. One kopek. Nobody has any money here. They deal in goods, barter. That's okay if they throw me a loaf of bread, but they won't do that. You have to be a businessman to work this market."

And, indeed, around them was a busy marketplace with people making small deals in all corners. An old man traded a leather purse for a beard comb made of palm. A piece of cloth was traded for an old cabbage. The little commerce that was done was totted on the abacus. But nowhere were the stands of fruits and vegetables that had once been seen in Moscow. Alex thought that was strange, since this was the south where all good things grew.

"The drought," Ivan said. "They lost their crops in the drought. I think we can starve here almost as well as we can in Moscow."

"At least we won't be cold doing it," Alex said, with a touch of the carefree *bezprizorni* spirit that he was beginning to feel from time to time—a feeling that what is, is.

Ivan was standing on his head again, spinning like a top. "What can I do?" Alex asked. "I don't know how to stand on my head."

"You be the caller," Ivan said. "Say, 'Come see the human spinning top.'"

"Come and see the human top," Alex called. "Come see the circus kid, star of the Moscow circus," he improvised.

Ivan laughed, and several people stopped and watched him whirling his legs, turning like a drunken windmill. This time two kopeks landed on the rug. Ivan folded himself up and rolled around like a rubber ball. Then he flattened himself out on the sidewalk and relaxed. The crowd dispersed.

"Do you know what I am doing?" he asked Alex. "I'll tell you. I am giving free entertainment to these *kulaks* and *muziks* who are eating a meal every day. I, Ivan, am giving charity. I am a philanthropist." He got up, picked up the kopeks, and pulled Alex into the crowd. Nearby an organ grinder was doing a little business with his parrot. For a kopek, the drowsy bird would pick a fortune from a pack the man held. For five kopeks the parrot would perform tricks, as the man kept announcing, but, for that service, there were no takers.

"I don't need a parrot to tell me my fortune," Ivan said. "Steal or starve, that's it."

Now they saw Peter making his way toward them. He was moving swiftly. "Let's go," he hissed, and Ivan and Alex whirled in their paths and followed. Behind them in the crowd, two policemen were craning their necks.

"Don't look back," Peter said. "They're after me. They just don't know it because they didn't see my face."

"What did you get?" Alex puffed, keeping up.

"Bread from the government store."

"You *stole* from the government store!" Ivan exclaimed. "What gall!" He laughed.

"What else can you do in this place!"

Back in the cave, Peter threw a loaf of bread to the Mongolian boy who was sitting at the entrance to be sure he got shares of everything coming into the cave. Miska, wrapped up in himself like a snail, was still sleeping.

"Get up," Peter said, prodding him gently. "Follow me."

Miska stumbled to his feet. "My stomach still hurts very much," he said. He looked pale, and dark circles made his eyes appear to sink way into his head.

"Never mind, now. Come on."

They left the cave and climbed farther up the hill. Kostia carried Miska when he fell far behind. Anya climbed like a little mouse on all fours.

"Where are we going?" Alex asked. "And why are we going?"

"Higher up," Peter said, "because we don't want to tangle with that crowd in the cave. I don't like their kind. They are not to be trusted."

"You're a lot of fools," Boris growled. "There is plenty of money to be had there. Do you think these boys in the cave are starving? Didn't you smell their soup last night? Didn't you see sausages hanging in the back of the cave?"

"We are going to have some soup ourselves," Peter answered. "Kostia and Leon have been out digging roots. The small boys have been getting grass and twigs for a fire."

They settled under a small outcropping of rocks—more like the caves Alex knew in the hills near his home.

"This is nothing compared to the big cave," Boris complained. "It is a big climb and when you get here what have you got!" He spat.

Peter said nothing, but the tension between him and Boris was growing, and it made the rest of them uneasy. Peter immediately set water to boil and made herb tea for Miska and one of the other boys who was complaining of bellyache. Miska curled up in a corner of the cave and stayed that way, whimpering from time to time.

Each day they went down to the town, and Ivan continued to do his whirling act while others stole small combs and pieces of leather, reselling them for a few kopeks. It was not like Moscow. You could not steal in one market and sell in another. Twice Peter made successful forays into the government store, returning to the cave with his shirt full of bread.

Boris and Grigory became more and more sullen. At night, Alex saw them slip out of the cave, more than once, returning in the morning, laughing, punching each other. Then one morning Peter caught them returning, reeling with drink.

"All right," Peter said. "This is the end. You must choose to stay with this band and keep its rules, or go with your new friends and stay with them. No more coming and going. Do you understand?"

"How can you be so stupid!" Boris shouted. "Don't you know that for taking a little cocaine over the mountain you can have enough money to buy your bread in the government store? And more. *We* have had sausage. *We* have had potatoes. Yes! We are no fools, my friend Grigory and me. We are professionals."

"Well, then," Peter said almost sadly, "you will have to do your business somewhere else. Good-bye, Boris. Good-bye, Grigory."

"It's time I went, anyway," Boris said. "I'm tired of hanging around with a bunch of children. We are going where there are grown men. Come on, Grigory." Grigory followed Boris obediently as he started down the hill. Alex thought Grigory looked doubtful, yet he knew he would go with Boris. He was like a shadow with almost no thoughts of his own.

The morning ritual began almost as if they were back in the bakery cellar in Moscow. Some boys tended the fire; one was in charge of cutting the bread into equal shares; and, as usual, the youngest boys were out gathering fuel for the fire. Anya usually went with the small boys to help as she could. They were just finishing the morning chores when Kostia spied Boris just below their ledge. "Look, there's Boris," he said. "He's come back. Perhaps he's not so crazy about his new friends, after all."

"Where?" Alex asked. "I don't see him."

"He was right there a minute ago," Kostia said. "I could see him waving his arm to Grigory."

"Shall we take him back, Peter?" Leon asked.

"Why not?" Peter said. "If he can live as the rest of us do."

Just then, where Boris's head had been, two strange heads appeared and then their bodies—two policemen from the village. "Don't move!" they shouted.

"All right," one said, as he approached. "We know who the robber is—the tall one. Stand up!" They approached Peter. "So, you think you can steal from the government store and get away with it." They laughed. "Not when you run with scum like this who will turn you in."

"These boys did not steal," Peter said, "and they did not turn me in, either. I think I know who did. Anyhow, you've got me, but you have nothing against these boys except that they are homeless like half the country."

"Don't tell us our duty," shouted one of the policemen. "We are told you are a bunch of smugglers, as well. On your feet, all of you. At least there will be a few less of you villains running around the town."

"Where will they take us?" Alex whispered nervously to Ivan.

"Not to heaven," Ivan said.

~10

When Alex saw the children's home, his first thought was: Why do we care so much if we are caught? Here is a real building to sleep in, after all this time sleeping in the cellar and the cave. They passed through locked gates, opened for them by a drowsy old man; then the policemen herded them into the entry and pulled a bell. The bell rang loudly in the courtyard. The boys were downcast and silent. Anya and Miska were crying and clinging to Peter. Peter, restless and angry, looked stony. The policemen muttered, cursed, and rang again. Finally a small old woman answered the door. Her face was in drapes of wrinkles, her eyes so light and pale in color they seemed transparent, her hair hidden beneath a ragged scarf.

"Not another load!" she grumbled. "Where am I supposed to put them? Can't this great new government build another shelter here?" This little woman looked like a grandmother, and Alex had expected a gentle voice. Instead, its deepness and roughness surprised him.

"Shut up, *babushka!*"* one of the policemen said. "You're lucky you don't get even more. The town is full of waifs very

* *babushka*—word for both scarf and grandmother

98

early this year because of the weather up north. You will just have to fit them in with a shoehorn."

The woman only grunted, and the policemen turned abruptly and left. "Quickly, quickly, stupid brats!" she cried to the children. "You are letting in all the cold air." And they followed her through the enormous door into a hall that was far colder than the outdoors because the sun never reached it. In the hall the air was almost unbreathable. Smoke and evil smells like a sewer were thick in the vestibule, and in another minute it became clear why.

The old woman looked at them. "I'm sure I have seen most of you scum before, so I don't have to waste my time. You know the rules here. And you know what will happen if you break them. Don't forget it! Now, get inside and find yourself a place." She unbarred the door and started to push them into the room beyond. "Wait!" she said. "Here! Is that one a girl? She goes to the other section." And she grabbed Anya, who cried out as the door slammed.

The scene that lay before them reminded Alex of a picture in *The Inferno*, a book that was on the shelves at his home in Kovrov. Like the cellar and the cave, the room was lit by small fires around which filthy children sat or lay. But the oily haze in the room was denser and the smells were more hideous, since efforts were made to stuff the broken windows with rags, and the smoke and stench were trapped inside with the children. Alex couldn't imagine how many were crammed in rough bunks, in corners, on window ledges. The floor was littered with bodies, and from some came cries and moans. Alex drew back at this sight, and Miska whimpered.

Since all the bunks were taken, with several children in a bunk, Peter led his dejected band to a dark corner, far from the fires, where fewer people were. They sank to the floor

99

and crouched there, getting their bearings, letting the events of the morning sink in.

In a while, the bar on the door was thrown, and the heavy door swung open. The director entered, conspicuously carrying a leather bludgeon.

"The *sooksin* is still here!" Peter whispered. "I thought he had been kicked out."

"Come forward, you boys who were just brought here."

"We have to go up," Kostia whispered to Alex, "or he will beat the whole roomful and then they'll point us out and they'll beat us up. So we will get beaten twice." Peter and his band stood and came to the door.

The director held a notebook. "Name?" he snapped, pointing at Kostia. "Next!" he snapped. "Next." One by one, they gave their names, their ages, places of birth. When he came to Peter, he said, "I know you, don't I? And this one and this one, too? You are too old for this shelter. In the morning, you will go with the police to prison and give us some room in here."

Hearing this, Miska, standing, but bright with his fever and weaving on his feet, cried out. "No! Don't send him away. No, don't." And he sprang forward, grabbing the director's coat in a piteous entreaty. "No, you can't! We will die without Peter."

The leather bludgeon in the director's hand was raised and brought down in one continuous heavy motion. A sound like rotted wood breaking, and Miska fell. Without another word, the director turned and walked out, slamming the door. It had taken only a moment . . . a flash in time.

Peter fell to his knees and gathered Miska up. "Make a place for him," he ordered, and his band pushed ahead of him, forcibly evicting two waifs from their bunk and laying

100

Miska upon it. Blood oozed from the place where the bludgeon had fallen. "Who has some vodka?" Peter shouted. "Come on, you pigs. Don't you think I know you have vodka? Give what you have or I will personally beat up each one of you."

A boy slowly detached himself from a group lying nearby and handed over a bottle with an inch of liquid in it. Peter sniffed it, put a drop on his tongue, and then poured it over the wound. Miska's breathing was so shallow it could scarcely be heard. "Kostia, Ivan, lie across his feet. Alex, lie on one side of him and I'll lie on the other. We'll try and keep him warm."

What had happened had left Alex feeling as if he himself had been struck. He felt a sympathetic pain in his head, and his heart palpitated as if he had been running. Even so, when the palpitations had eased somewhat, his fatigue led him finally into sleep, while he gave his body's warmth to the ailing child.

In the morning, Miska still had not opened his eyes, and his breathing was still shallow. Peter went to the barred door and banged on it. *"Babushka!"* he yelled. He did that over and over until, finally, the old woman came and opened the door.

"Stop the racket," she shouted. "Your gruel will get here when it will get here."

*"Chort tzdbya beeree!"** Peter shouted. "I don't give a damn about the filthy swill. There is a terribly sick and injured child in here. He needs help. Medicines. Tell the director."

"Look who is giving orders!" the old woman snorted. The

* the devil with you

101

door slammed, and Peter went back to watching Miska, snarling and cursing in a way that was not like the Peter they knew.

A little later, a bucket of gray gruel was brought in by the old woman and the old man who guarded the gate. The waifs rushed or shuffled over to it and dipped into the bucket with their own bowls.

"Did you tell the director?" Peter demanded.

"I told him," she answered.

"Yes! Well, what did he say?"

"What do you think?" she snapped.

"The old sot!" Peter exploded. "The old *dryan*! He's probably still in his feather bed in a vodka sleep."

"Don't scream at *me*," the old woman said. "I'm just an old woman who has to live, too. I do my job."

"You know," Ivan said, coming up and speaking to her very sweetly, "you're almost like a real human being." Then he barked, "They just forgot to give you a heart."

"A good thing, too," the matron said. "If I had one, you thieves would cut it out and eat it." Some of the boys laughed.

"Why, the old bitch is just like a dear ugly mother to me," a waif said, sidling up to her. "She doesn't need a heart. All she needs is to know how to cook up a pot of soup or gruel. That's what she's good for." The old woman kicked him away.

"Please," Peter now begged, "this child is badly hurt."

The old woman looked around the room. "Which one is he?" she barked.

"Here," Peter said, leading her to the bunk where Miska still lay without moving.

"He looks no better or worse than the rest of you," she said. "He's sleeping."

"His head is opened," Peter said. "The wound will fester without proper dressing, and he was so sick with fever when he came. He is sleeping, yes, but he doesn't awaken."

"What do you want me to do?" the woman asked. She sounded almost reasonable. "Everyone is sick." Where had Alex heard that before? From Miska, he thought, when he first arrived in the cellar. The old woman shuffled away. "They get better or they don't," she said.

"Tell the director," Peter shouted, furious again. "Tell that pig of a director that the child he struck last night needs a doctor."

"Doctor!" she laughed, and opened the door. Even the waifs who had been paying not much attention to the furor in the corner snickered at that but did not distract themselves more than a moment from their aimless pursuits: smoking, playing cards, drowsing, catching lice.

"And while you are at it," Peter shouted, "tell him that if he sends me to the police, I will tell the commissars a thing or two that he has done now and in the past."

"I would like to go out and find Boris and poke out his eyes," Kostia said.

"What will happen to Boris now will be a big punishment," Peter said. "He will live in that cave with those criminals, perhaps all his days."

Once again, Alex allowed himself to think about the future. How, he wondered, will the rest of us live out all our days? It came to him almost as a new fright that he could not see past living in a cellar or a cave, being caught and brought to this pest house.

103

A few of the waifs in the shelter had pulled themselves to their feet, squeezed through the broken windows and out into the courtyard behind the building. Alex could see them hoisting each other over the wall and pulling up the last companion.

"But if they can get out, why do they come back?" Alex exclaimed. "Why are we staying here?"

"Don't worry. As soon as Miska is better, we'll get out," Kostia said. "We have to pick our time, though. As for these others, most of them don't care about being free on their own. All they want is a place to flop with vodka and cocaine."

"This place is a laugh compared to Moscow," Kostia said. "In Moscow, when they get you in, it's harder to get away."

"Is it as bad as this?" Alex asked. "So . . . terrible."

"They're all terrible," Peter said.

"In Moscow," Leon said, "there is one shelter where they have real cots. You sit at a table for supper and they give you a spoon to eat with. You have a bath sometimes. They give you some clothes. But it is just like being in a cage. They are always bringing in foreigners to see you, to show how perfect the shelter is and what good care the government takes of you. There was nothing at all to do there. Even so, if they were all like that, it wouldn't be so bad. Once, I even tried to get back in there in the freezing weather, but they only take a few."

All day, they watched over Miska. Kostia and Ivan went over the wall and came back hours later with a loaf of bread and a bottle of vodka.

"Don't tell me how you got it," Peter said. "I'm afraid I know."

"Please, comrade," Ivan said, crossing his eyes and putting

on another of his shows. "Please, comrade, my little brother has a terrible fever. Will you kindly give me that loaf of bread you are carrying, and also that bottle of vodka?"

"Oh, surely, my boy!" Kostia said, sticking out his stomach and pretending to be a fat old man. "Take it and take these rubles, too, so that you may buy your little brother some medicine for his fever."

"Don't worry," Ivan said to Peter, "we only knocked him over. He wasn't even hurt."

When night came, the matron and the old gatekeeper entered with a bucket of bean soup, thin, wicked, and sour, but hot. Babushka ladled it into their bowls as they crowded around her, taking their insults and their taunts with a choking laugh or with a rough return of her own. Occasionally, she would give a quick shove to one of the boys who crowded her or abused her, and the strength of those small arms was astounding. Even a big and swarthy lad was thrown upon his back.

"That one is made of iron," Kostia said. "Don't tangle with her."

Boys returned through the windows, carrying bottles of vodka, cigarettes, and other things. Night fell. The noise, the smoke, the odors, the hateful atmosphere made Alex wish to go through one of those windows by himself. If one could go, why stay with this unsavory band? But he now felt it would be like leaving his family.

It was during his turn to keep Miska warm, sometime in the deep night, that he sensed a difference—a strange silence, a suspension. It was nothing you could say that you heard or did not hear, felt or did not feel. It was simply *known*. Fear engulfed Alex, and he awakened Peter.

"Peter, come and see Miska!"

Peter leapt up and came to the bunk where Miska lay, as he had lain for over a day and night. He knelt beside him, felt his hands, his head, put his face to his chest and his mouth. Then he banged his fist against the hard floor and put his face in his hands. When, finally, Peter raised his head, Alex could see, in the pale oily glow of the fires, that his face was contorted, his fists clenched and striking the air. Then he reached over and covered Miska's face with the rags that were covering his body, touching him gently. Alex did not need Peter to tell him. He had known even before he called that the light, burning low in Miska, had gone out. Died.

Peter went over to where the others of the band lay, shaking them awake, one by one. "Come," he said hoarsely. "We're going now. Miska is . . . dead." His voice sounded strangled as he said it, even though he said it in a hard way, a rough way. The strange light in the cavernous room lit the sleeping children. Cries, coughs, groans tore holes in the oily haze as Peter, his mind smoking like the fire, his soul grinding in hatred and anger, led his little band through the maze of bodies to the window, signaling them to be silent. They eased through the window, tearing their already torn rags on the rough edges, scraping their flesh, and found themselves in the courtyard, patterned by the dark shadows of the wall.

"Start going over and wait for me just outside the far corner of the wall. Now hurry."

"Where are you going?" Kostia asked.

"Never mind. I have something to do."

"We'll do it with you," Ivan said.

"No, I have to do it alone. Be quiet now, or you'll spoil everything."

He watched them cross the dark courtyard, then turned and ran to a corner of the building where a stone drainpipe rose to the floor above. He was up it like a serpent, then into the corridor, quietly moving, holding himself against the wall, sinking into the shadows when he heard a sound. Then, so quietly that he might have been doing this in a dream, he turned a doorknob and let himself into the room where the director snored in his feather bed, his bludgeon by his side, his stove burning brightly, and his enormous brass samovar steaming.

In one leap, Peter was beside the bed and had grabbed the bludgeon, poking the ugly man awake with it. "*Svolotch*," Peter hissed. "Wake up. Wake, you, you *dryan*. Here you lie in your featherbed, with your stove nearby, while below, sick children"—his voice caught here—"freeze, starve, die. I have seen you and your wickedness for many years, and you are even less a human being than you ever were. Now I am going to fix your brutal hands so that you cannot maim another child for a long time." And he raised the bludgeon.

The director had lain there seemingly paralyzed, his mouth and eyes wide open, but now he lunged, his great fat hands closing around Peter's throat, letting out a scream as he did so. Immediately, Peter dropped the bludgeon to try and release the strangling grip, but the man was stronger than his soft flesh would suggest. The two, locked in a struggle, thrashed about, Peter venting the hate of years as his hands fell on the ugly man's face.

The director's cries brought the old woman to the door. She too cried out but watched the fight, not moving. The two combatants now crashed off the bed onto the floor, the weight of their bodies causing them to roll, one on top of the other, until they were stopped suddenly by the legs of the heavy table holding the samovar. The force caused the heavy brass vessel to teeter. For a moment, it balanced precariously on the edge, then fell with a terrible crash, spilling its boiling contents on the director, its enormous weight landing on his head. The grasp released.

Peter's arms were scalded. He pulled them back, but the release of the hands on his throat gave such relief that the pain of the burns was not immediately felt. The old woman held her hands over her mouth, staring with horror at the director, who did not move. Now Peter, gasping for breath, looked at him. He leaned forward and put his face near the man's mouth. He raised the eyelids, listened to his heart. The man was dead.

Peter stood. He moved quickly toward the doorway. The old woman shrank back, holding herself from him. Then Peter started to run. He let himself out and down the same way he had come. In the background, the old woman's voice could now be heard calling for help. But Peter did not immediately make for the corner of the wall where the rest of the band waited. Instead, he ran around the building to the side opposite.

Pushing some rags from a window, he hoisted himself in. Then he started to search a room that was much like the one they had all just left, except smaller. He moved up and down the rows of children, sometimes turning one over. He stood for a moment in the middle of the room, slowly scanning the shadows, trying to ignore the cries that came from some of the bodies. It took him several minutes more, but then he found her. Anya was curled like a kitten on a window ledge, sleeping soundly. He lifted her gently and hurried to the window he had entered, whispering to her as he moved.

"Anya, it's me, Peter. We're leaving here. Wake up now."
He thrust her through the window and climbed after her.
She was still weaving with sleep, but she followed him across
the courtyard.

Ivan was waiting, his head just appearing above the far
side of the wall. When he saw them approaching, he let
himself down by his toes, clinging like a trapeze artist, and
Peter handed Anya to him. Then, with Ivan's help, Peter
quickly went over the wall himself. In the background,
lights were being lit, and the alarmed voices of the old
woman and then the old man could be heard.

"Follow me," Peter now said. "Quickly!" And they were
running silently along the walls, then down the sleeping
streets to the outskirts of the town. Across the dark fields
they ran, frightening the mice. The night sounds of the
Caucusus came to them over the rolling field, from the rocky
crags—the restlessness of birds and animals, rivers turning,
tree limbs cracking—but also the night brought a quiet that
made Alex think of old Tolka and the nights he had spent in
the quiet woods. "You can hear the ferns growing," Tolka
used to say. "You can hear the snakes shedding their skins."

Now they started their ascent, stumbling in the dark as
they climbed the foothills. As yet, nobody had spoken. No
one said what was in their hearts. But when they came to a
place far from the children's shelter, an hour's climb for a
mountain goat, they rested, throwing themselves on the
stony ground to regain their breath.

Then Peter said, "Miska was murdered by the brute director. Now I have killed the murderer."

They all stared at him, not believing it. "Do you understand me?" Peter said, almost tonelessly. "I have killed him."

Anya, who had been weeping softly ever since she had

been told by Ivan of Miska's death, now stopped crying and said firmly, "Good."

"I have not wanted to kill anyone in my life," Peter said. He shook his head again and again, as if he could not believe that this had happened. "No," he said, as if reassuring himself. "With killing everywhere, I did not want to kill. What would Jacob, the baker, say to me now! But I have caused this man's death, and I will have to pay for it somehow. Certainly they will look for me, and then they will arrest me."

"No," Kostia said quickly. "We will leave this place. . . . They won't find you. We will go back to Moscow."

"Yes, what will you eat there?" Peter asked.

"It can't stay frozen forever."

"No, just long enough for you to starve."

"Then, at last, we will have to play a rougher game," Leon said.

"No," Peter said emphatically.

"What do you mean, no?" Leon asked. "You just said you killed a man."

"Not for food, and I do not mean to do it again. It was an accident, but even so, I killed him."

Alex had been hearing this as if he were floating high above it, a witness. Despite the exhausting run from the shelter, and the astounding and shocking thing he had just heard from Peter, his mind seemed clearer than it had been in months.

"If I were head of a government," he said, "I would not allow thousands of children to run around in rags and starve, having to steal and even kill to stay alive. The first thing I would do—the very first thing—would be to see that the children got food and a warm place to sleep."

"Like a children's shelter, maybe?" Kostia said sarcastically. "Like a lovely children's shelter with a fatherly director like that one? Ha! Let me tell you something, dreamer: As soon as the government does something for you, you are a slave. The *bezprizoni* are not slaves, at least."

"There are places where it is different," Alex said, with sudden assurance.

"How do you know?" Kostia said. "How do you know that all places are not the same, where people are slaves of the government?"

"Because my teacher, Katriana Sergyeva, told me so."

"Listen," Leon said. "It is the same here, with the Czar or with the Bolsheviks—the people have nothing. They are not free."

"But we are free," Kostia said. "We are free."

It surprised Alex to hear his own voice, out here in the bright night of the Caucusus. It was as if the confusion had suddenly been lifted, and, in seeing the present, he saw the possibilities of the future.

"Okay," he said. "You are right. We are free. But what can we do with our freedom?"

"What kind of nonsense is that?" Kostia asked. "We can do anything we want."

"But what do we want?" Alex said. "Do we want to spend the rest of our lives doing nothing but trying to find food, freezing, wearing filthy rags?" It was the first time he had brought these thoughts forward, even to himself. In the back of his mind, he had thought of this period with the band as a little piece of time, a transition between his old life in Kovrov and the unknown future. Now he was saying, if this is the future, I do not want it. "No," he said, more to himself than to anyone else. "There has to be something else."

111

And like an echo from the hills of his mind there played back to him the voice of Katriana: *There must be someplace better.*

"I wouldn't like to live another way," Leon said. "No Bolsheviks, no Czar, tell me what to do and what kind of crops to grow. I have no house for them to burn. I go where I want. I am a traveler and an explorer."

"*Chort tzdbya beeree!*" Ivan said. "You dunce, you. Don't you remember anymore what it is like to live with a family? To do tricks on a high wire with your family? That is better than this freedom. Many times."

Through all of this, Peter had been sitting, clenching and unclenching his burned hands, occasionally thrusting his head into his hands or staring off into the darkness. Now a silence grew and spread among them, and it was full of fear for Peter, full of grief for Miska. It was unspoken, as they kicked pebbles, dug heels into hard dirt, but it was there.

Thinking of Miska now, Alex had a sudden vision of a white funeral he had seen for a young child. A small cart with white pillars carried the coffin, and on the cart a young girl sat holding a gold ikon. Behind the cart, a priest walked, intoning psalms. Today, such funerals were not allowed for the people. But he had once seen a red funeral for an important town official. There was a large scarlet hearse with gold columns, and six outriders with orange coats and cocked hats. There were red flags and trumpets, drums, cymbals, and red flowers. Pictures like these stayed in his mind, as pictures remain in a storybook.

And the mourning that they were doing now was like a funeral, Alex thought, but not a funeral. He wandered a little way into the night by himself, thinking of the small, rag-wrapped foot beneath the barrow as he had first seen it, the eager face listening to him reading, the cold blue hands tending his fever and giving him tea. Now that the high tension of the escape was behind them, this time to think gave him the kind of pain that he'd felt when his family was gone—the feeling of things stopping. Could that first loss have been only months ago—not years? He felt so much older.

~11

Resting, waiting for Peter to take the lead once more, to become Peter again and direct them, the boys curled and sprawled among the rocks.

Peter withdrew within himself. First he walked to the edge of a small brook and soaked his scalded forearms in the cold water. Then he walked to the cliff's edge, starting one way, turning, starting another—restless, inconsolable.

Alex thought, that's the way I felt the day I ran to Katriana, not knowing what to do. But there was no Katriana for Peter. Thinking of her now, Alex's mind roamed back through that day, and it all spoke to him as if it were a book being read or a magic lantern show. He saw her in her little room, eyes shining, voice gentle, soothing him, telling him not to despair, telling him of her dreams, giving him hope. Now Alex walked over to Peter impulsively.

"Peter," he said hesitantly, "I have a good friend—you have heard me speak of my teacher, Katriana Sergyeva." His voice caught when he spoke her name. Once again, speech brought reality to thoughts. "Once, on the day I was left alone, she told me about places in the world where people are free, even in their houses, where they own their land and keep their crops. Where they go about as they like, even if they do not live as we do. Peter, we could all go to some place like that where no one could catch you. I have an uncle who went to America. He lives in a big city called New York."

"America!" Peter replied. "That's across the ocean! And how do you know it is different than this?"

"Katriana knows. She only tells the truth."

"Well, that may be the truth or not," Peter said. "But even if it was true, we have no way to get there."

"If there was such a place, would you want to be there?" Alex pressed.

"Perhaps," was all Peter would say.

"Peter," Alex went on now, as thoughts deep in the back of his mind spilled forth. "Katriana Sergyeva has a brother in Petrograd."

"You mean Leningrad," Peter said.

"Yes, I forget that is its name now. Even Katriana says Petrograd or St. Petersburg. But let me tell you: The brother can help people who want to go to such places, Katriana says. She wanted to go herself, but she was not able to."

Peter looked up. "Your *teacher* wanted to go away?"

"Yes."

"She wanted to leave when she had a home and work and food?"

"But she said that is not all. She said that the thoughts have to be free."

"Yes," Peter said. "I think that, too. Perhaps I like your Katriana Sergyeva."

"Katriana says it is not her Russia now. Maybe sometime, but not now."

"Did you want to go away, too?" Peter asked.

Alex thought about it. "I didn't take it seriously then. All I could think of was that my family was gone. And I didn't think of it again until just now. But now, with the police looking for you, and then because of what happened to Miska . . ." He choked as he said that, and both looked away. Then he went on. "Well, there are all these. . . ." He motioned to the children lying on the hill. "It could happen to them, too. To us, too."

Peter nodded. Then he said, "Do you know where this brother can be found?"

"Yes. At least, I think so, if he is still at the same place. Katriana told me where he was working. But how can we get all the way to Petrograd . . . I mean Leningrad, with the police after you?"

Peter said, "Haven't you learned *anything* yet? Then we might have to leave you behind."

That deflated Alex a little, but at the same time he was elated that Peter sounded more like Peter again. They were not, after all, set adrift with no one to lead them. And, too, he heard the echo of his own voice speaking to Peter, informing him, and it surprised him. If they did go to Leningrad and perhaps leave the country, all these children would go because he had thought of it. It amazed him that he might be affecting someone else's actions, someone's choices, when he had scarcely ever been asked to make one for himself.

Once again, Peter had begun pacing about, walking alone, head down, but the sun had not yet risen when he returned to the group, saying, "Everyone up. We're off."

"I'm hungry," Anya said. "I want to find some food first."

"Later," Peter said.

"Where will we go?" Leon asked.

"What difference!" Peter said, almost lightly.

116

Only Alex knew there might truly be a destination. It pleased him.

By midday they were high in the mountains. The steep, craggy paths slowed their progress, but they felt safer at these heights where the lazy police might not bother to climb. They were in snow now, and, when they stopped to rest, they sat at the edge of a gorge below which a river wove whitely. In the distance, above the cliffs and forests, an eagle flew in and out of clouds.

And they were not alone in these hills. When Alex first saw shadowy figures along the paths, he feared it was the police, but they were a hardy people called the Ingushes. "After the revolution, they did not want to join the collectives," Peter said, "so they left the villages and went into the mountains. Now they keep on fighting the revolutionaries, even though the war is over. They raid, steal, ambush the GPU squads, set fire to collective farms. They keep their cattle hidden way up here."

"They look . . . wild," Alex whispered. And they did, with their matted hair, savage-looking beards, enormous sheepskin caps that made them look like some kind of beasts.

"Maybe we look pretty wild ourselves," Peter said. "They won't bother us unless we try to take their cattle."

"Would they give us just a little milk?" Anya asked. "How I would love some milk!"

"Don't you think of anything but food?" Kostia asked.

"No," Anya said.

"Look," Alex said to her, "did you know you can eat this?" And, as old Tolka had shown him, he stripped a piece of bark from the white birches. Carefully he peeled off the papery outer layer and, from the inside, peeled a thin fibrous piece, which he gave to Anya. She popped it into her mouth, made a face, but chewed it happily. Soon the others were doing the same, and their progress was slowed now for a raid on the birch trees.

"Come on," Peter said. "We can't hang around here too long or we will get the Ingushes' attention. They probably think these are their trees. Put some bark in your shirts and take it along." So they proceeded, chewing birch bark.

By late afternoon they were tired, and Alex and Ivan were carrying a sleepy Anya. "This one is a nuisance," Ivan said. "Let's throw her over." They made a swing of Anya, who screamed a mock scream.

"No, don't," Kostia said. "She might be good to eat later." Anya chuckled. These three watched her like a treasure. She understood their banter. In the cold, in the misery, she was comfortable with them.

"They will watch the railroad stations on this side of the mountain," Peter said. "So we'll stay here tonight. Not many bands will be traveling north now, so we will stick out. We will have to make a plan in the morning."

They built a fire of fallen branches and warmed themselves while they melted snow. Once again, old Tolka's teaching came to serve Alex and the band. They dug beneath the snow to find the dead leaves that had fallen in autumn. Then they lay, back to back, covering themselves in the leafy blanket. In the distance, and sometimes even closer at hand, the howls of wolves could be heard, but to these children it was not the most frightening thing they had heard. Indeed, Alex thought, in the months that had just passed, he had slept in worse places.

* * *

In the morning, they dug for roots beneath the snow and chewed on more birch bark. Then they followed Peter across the crest of the mountain and climbed cautiously down the other side. In the distance, below them, the railroad could be seen. "I don't think they'll be watching here," Peter said, "but we'd better be careful. We'll go down until we're right above the station. When we see the train in the distance, we will speed down, a couple at a time, not as a band. Then wait for the train to leave. Don't get on until it's moving. We could be trapped in those boxes if they see us."

They waited, resting on the sun-warmed slope, warming their bodies from the cold night. Anya and some of the other younger children dug for green shoots beneath the earth, munching away the hours. Then, "Here it comes," one of them shouted.

They waited as the train chugged into the station and discharged its passengers. They watched the platform for any groups of police, but saw only one local policeman in sloppy attire, trying to keep his eyes in four directions. When the second bell rang, Peter called, "Now!" and they sprinted down the hillside, leaping as if they were on springs, stones clattering to the gulch below, and entered the station yard singly, in twos, or threes, just as the train got slowly underway. When it was out of the station they ran for it, covered by the train itself from the eyes of the policeman. They grabbed the outside handholds, swung up onto the roof, passing Anya and the little ones up. Then they rode, spread-eagled, on the roof, flying through the countryside on the way to Moscow.

It was almost two hours before they arrived at the next station, and, as the train slowed, steam rising about them from the engine, they slipped down over the sides of the cars and ran alongside, arriving at the station just as the train pulled in and its passengers descended. Peter collared one of the small boys as he started to beg.

"Fool!" he hissed. "We are still being invisible," and he led him and the others to the side of the station away from the eyes of the stationmaster and the patrolling soldiers.

"I'm hungry," the boy protested.

"Oh, what news!" Kostia said, and gave him a kick.

But Anya was loose like a wound-up toy. She ran around picking up scraps that people dropped, like a bird in a park. Then she stood staring at a woman eating a piece of cake, her great blue eyes wide, her small mouth quivering, licking her lips as the woman swallowed. The woman turned away with a frown and a shake of her head. Then she turned back and gave what remained to Anya. It was gone in a gulp, and Anya was off to stare at someone else. Alex grabbed her. "Cut it out, Anya!" And he whisked her to the side of the station where the rest of the band rested behind baggage carts.

When the train started up again, they made a run for the black boxes beneath the carriages. Their return to Moscow was like their escape to the south, long and tedious, and, instead of gradually getting warmer, it became colder. When they were far enough away from the mountains to feel safe, they emerged to forage at the stations, the little ones begging, Ivan doing his headstands with Alex announcing the event, and the others doing what they did best to find food and drink.

"I'm glad we're going back to Moscow, even if it's cold," Kostia said. "Moscow is where everything happens. Every day there is something new."

"We're not going back to stay in Moscow," Peter now said.

Alex wondered if he had only just made up his mind, or if he had decided back in the mountains, which seemed like months ago instead of days ago.

"Then where are we going?"

"For now, we are going to Leningrad." He seemed to be telling them no more than they needed to know at the moment.

"Leningrad is okay," Leon said. "Leningrad is almost as good as Moscow. But why don't we just stay in Moscow? We're almost there now. I'm sick of the trains."

"I'm sick of them, too," Anya said.

"We'll just see if there isn't something good in Leningrad," Peter said firmly.

"Peter's getting too bossy," Leon said under his breath to Kostia.

"You don't have to go if you don't want to," Kostia said belligerently. "You only have to stay with Peter if you want to. Me, I'll try Leningrad."

At Moscow they had to change stations, running through the familiar snowy street, happy to be free of the confinement of the trains, jumping, leaping to vent their pent-up spirits.

"The trip to Leningrad is short," Peter said. "This is the easy part."

And thus cheered and encouraged, they waited for the early morning train to Leningrad, avoiding the bands who dominated the stations, staying out of fights for territory. "But I can get food here," Anya complained when she was kept from begging.

"You can also get a broken nose here, so wait a while," Kostia told her.

They had to wait the night in the station because there

121

was no train until morning, but time was something that had no beginning and no end. They did not count it, only what it produced for them, and this time it gave them rest from the tiresome travel in the black boxes.

It was early afternoon when they found themselves standing on the Nevsky Prospekt in Leningrad, not far from the Winter Palace, home of the Czars. The ride had been only six hours, a mere blink in time. They followed Peter to the Touchkoff Quay on the river Neva, still frozen near its banks, where ice fishermen stood. Down the steps of the quay they went, holding close to the stone walls until they found a shelter in the embankment itself. There they settled as they always did, easing their bodies around rocks and stones, dirt and clay, to make a temporary abode.

Alex took Peter aside. "Shall we try to find Basil Sergyevitch Sokolov immediately?" Alex asked.

"As quickly as possible," Peter said, "because I must tell the rest what is happening very soon."

"Why not tell them now?" Alex said.

"I did not want to raise their hopes or else start an argument, if we were not sure ourselves what could be done."

Alex now noted that three of the boys were not there, but shortly, Leon and two other boys returned with three fish taken from the pail of an ice fisherman.

They ate the fish raw. Alex gagged but felt nourished when he had choked it down. Anya had no trouble, sucking the little bones. "In my old band," she said, "we cooked a rat for supper many nights, but we did not have to eat raw fish."

Alex laughed. He was thinking about scorched oatmeal again.

122

"We can't all go to see your teacher's brother," Peter said quietly to Alex. "They'd throw us out. They'd report us. Here, let me see you." He pulled Alex over. "You still have your boots, eh? Well, that's something." He ran up the step of the quay to the street, then down the curb to where a horse-drawn cart awaited the return of its driver. Peter bent down and scooped up some grease from the wheel, then returned to the embankment. He spread the grease on Alex's boots, buffing it with the ragged sleeve of his shirt. "Look at that!" Peter said. "Like new! You could sell those for a good dinner right now."

Alex held up his feet, exhibiting the soles. Enormous holes took up most of the space where soles should have been. "Not too good a dinner," he laughed.

"This may not be a bad place for food," Leon said. "It's better than Moscow, anyway. There are all these fish in the river. I think you are right, Peter, after all. I think we should stay here at least until it warms up in Moscow."

Peter said, "Well then, I am going to tell you that we did not come to Leningrad to stay. We came here to find someone who may help us leave Russia."

Silence. Only the clink and chop of the ice fisherman nearby. Then: "Leave Russia!" Kostia spoke for them all.

"Alex knows of someone who knows about this," Peter said. "He is going to see him now."

"But I don't want to leave Russia," Leon said. "And I'm telling you we should not have much trouble getting fish."

"We would not be going only because it is hard to find food," Peter said. "We would go because . . . because . . ."

"Because now we are boys who are stealing and may have to go to a children's home," Alex said. "But one day, soon, we will be men who are stealing, and we will go to prison for the rest of our lives. We would be going because nothing else but this is going to happen to us all our lives."

There was silence. Then Leon said, "But can't you give Leningrad a chance? It's not bad." A few of the small boys agreed.

"Think about it," Peter said. "No one would have to go who does not want to."

Anya went down to the river's edge and ladled water into her bowl. "Wash your hands," she directed Alex.

"Ouch!" Alex cried. "It's freezing!"

"Put your face in it," Anya ordered. "Wash it."

Alex did as she told him. Now several children climbed over Alex like mother monkeys, picking off dirt, lint, hay, grass, cinders. Anya stood on Kostia's shoulders and arranged Alex's hair, strand by strand, then beat his cap in the air and laid it carefully on his head. She regarded him proudly. "Isn't he beautiful," she said. She leaned over and kissed him. A lump choked Alex's throat. How long since anyone had kissed him, told him he was "beautiful"!

"You'll get by," Peter said. "We'll wait right here. Now go."

～12

Alex was off, along the quay to the Nevsky Prospekt, looking for Fontanka Street, which Katriana had told him was not far from the Winter Palace, but he had gone nearly a mile and had not seen it. He had just begun to worry that the name of Fontanka Street had been changed, as so many had, when he saw it—the fine old Anitchkoff Palace, now being used as a museum and library, the former home of the Dowager Empress.

Now he found himself frightened by the idea of entering the building—the only building he had been in, in months, except for the stations, the bakery cellar, and the children's home. Surely they would see him as a street waif and thief and throw him down the steps head first. Nevertheless, he climbed the steps, dusting his clothes as he went, straightening his cap.

He entered an enormous, dark, quiet vestibule. In the corners, stone statuary. On the walls, dark paintings in heavy frames. But no people, no books. Surely there would be books in a library. Cautiously he moved forward until he stood in the center of the hall. Then a voice, echoing as if in a tunnel, said, "Yes? May I help you?"

Alex was startled. It frightened him more than if the voice had said, "Get out of here, you ragamuffin!" He didn't reply

125

but looked around warily. He had no idea where the voice was coming from.

"Are you looking for something in particular?"

There it was. The voice came from a little old woman, no bigger than he was. She was seated in a dark corner, knitting. How could she see in the dark?

Alex cleared his throat. "Yes, please. I am looking for someone."

"Come over, please. I can't see well, but I can hear very plainly. I can hear a whisper." Alex moved to the corner, and the woman peered through her heavy glasses. Her eyes seemed to be in tunnels of glass. "Now, who was it you wanted?"

"I am looking for Basil Sergyevitch Sokolov. He works in the library."

"Yes, yes, I know. He is the one who drags one foot and has the very cold hands. That man must have no gloves. Oh dear, there goes my ball of wool. Could I trouble you to find it for me? I'm nearly blind. By the time I find it, it will be unwound across the hall." Alex picked it up and handed it to her. "Oh, your hands are cold, too. I guess you have lost your gloves, as well."

"Yes," Alex said. "That's right. But do you know where I can find Basil Sergyevitch?"

"You can go through those double doors over there and into the big room beyond. He will be one of the young men behind the long table."

Alex thanked the old woman and crossed the hall to the dark wooden door, polished like a mirror. How long since he had been in such a place! He opened it cautiously with the elaborate brass knob and found himself in an enormous room with shelves of books and papers. Here and there, some men pored over large volumes, but none of these men could be Basil. They were too old.

At a very long table, two younger men were sorting papers. They raised their heads as Alex entered, and he dropped his eyes. Beneath the table he could see their feet. If one of these was Basil, would he have the fine, polished old leather boots or the high black shoes? Alex looked up. They had gone back to their paperwork. One had a sweet face like Katriana's, but he was very blond. The other had a round, serious face, but his hair was like the dark oak of the door. Katriana's was, too, Alex remembered very well. He eased closer to the desk, walking on his tiptoes so as not to disturb anyone.

"Yes?" the fair young man asked sharply. Alex felt fearful and confused. He had not planned what to say. "Yes? May I help you?" the man asked, looking Alex in the eye, then craning his neck to see him more completely.

Alex felt he was being sized up and recognized for what he was. "I . . . er . . . am looking for . . . a geography book," he said, his tongue doing the thinking.

"A geography book!" Was that so dreadful to ask for? "What kind of geography book?"

"A geography book of . . . of Russia, comrade."

"Ah, well, of course all the geography books will have outdated maps now. There has not yet been time to have the maps show the new names of cities and so forth."

"Oh, I see," Alex said. Was this man Basil? How could he know? Could he ask further questions? He knew, somehow, that it was wisest not to, so he said only, "Thank you, comrade," and hurried out of the room. Was the other man

Basil? Had he failed in his very important mission? He did not know.

He waited now across the street from the Anitchkoff Palace, stamping his feet to keep them from going numb, waiting for the young men to emerge at the end of their working day. He clapped his hands together and blew on them. How reliable the body was, always to be able to produce hot breath no matter how cold it was.

And then, there was the man he had spoken to, walking hurriedly down Fontanka Street. This was not Basil. Alex knew it at once. The workers in the palace straggled out, one or two at a time, and when he thought they had all left and he must, somehow, have missed the man he sought, the great doors opened and a figure swathed in a heavy coat and a fur hat that covered his hair came slowly down the stairs. He paused at the bottom and then proceeded to walk down the street toward the embankment. He dragged one foot badly.

Alex leaped forward and came up behind him. "Please, sir, may I speak with you?"

The man did not turn around. "Please, sir," Alex said a little louder. "I am a friend of Katriana Sergyeva. . . ."

The man continued walking, but he spoke without turning around. "Just follow me. Don't speak anymore. Stay back a little, and then approach me when I stop."

Alex did what he was told. He let the man, who he now felt sure was Basil, get several yards ahead and then followed him until they reached the banks of the Neva. There Basil stopped and went over to the embankment. He looked over his shoulders in both directions, then nodded.

Alex approached. "I'm Alex, sir. Katriana was my teacher, and she told me to come and see you."

"I thought possibly it was me that you wanted in the library," Basil said. "But I couldn't speak to you. I hoped you'd wait. Yes, Katriana spoke of you."

"Katriana! Have you seen her, then?"

"Yes, she has been to Leningrad."

"Is she *here*?" Alex could not hold in his excitement.

"No, she isn't."

"Then has she done what she wanted to do?" Alex asked eagerly.

"Yes, she has!"

"But that's what I wish to do now! Where is Katriana?" Alex had not dared to dream that he might see her again. He was in such a stir he almost forgot his main mission.

"She is in another country, helping others," Basil said, looking around nervously.

"Could I go there?"

"I would have to see. I think it might be arranged. I have a friend with a small boat."

Now Alex remembered. "But sir, I am not alone."

"Ah, did you find your family, then? That's splendid!"

Alex thought. "Not exactly," he said. "These are other boys like myself, and a girl as well."

"Other students from Kovrov?" He was surprised.

"No sir, they are just children with no homes, no families, like me."

"And where are they?"

"They are close by here, down at the embankment."

"You go ahead, and I will follow behind. We must be very careful."

Alex hurried ahead. There were few pedestrians on the Touchkoff Quay at this hour. The cold wind that blew from the river discouraged loitering, but there was a scattering of soldiers and regular police in their black uniforms and red caps. A priest walked slowly along the river, his robes, formerly black, now green with age. Alex waited a moment till all these had passed by, then looked back to see if Basil was in sight. Then he sped down the stairs to the lower embankment where the boys were still huddled together, some dozing, some playing cards. They were instantly awake and standing. "What did he say?" Kostia asked.

But Alex had no time to answer because Basil had just reached the last step. "Oh, Lord!" he said, looking at the boys, lined up now as if for an army inspection. From the look on his face Alex could see he was not pleased with what he saw. What had he expected? Alex had told him that his friends were homeless just as he was. He looked at the group. How used to this filthy ragtag appearance he had become. It was he, with his grease-polished boots and brushed coat, who looked odd and out of place. Had Basil expected other threadbare, but washed and brushed boys?

"Alex," Basil said, "these are a great many. Too many for the little boat. We can take you. We can take another one or two. The others, later, perhaps. I have never sent so many at once."

"But I can't leave them," Alex said. "It was my idea to come here. I can't leave them now. They are my friends." And, yes, he thought, my family.

Basil said, "I will have to go home and think. I will meet you here tomorrow at the same time." He left them.

They ate the bread that Leon had found earlier, and then, once again, they huddled together for the night, now watching heavy barges crawling through the ice-clogged Neva, the floes crunching, the lanterns of the ships wavering and blinking. To see it, to feel the quiet of the city night, one would think all was well, all was right.

In the morning, they dispersed to ply the streets, to forage. There were plenty of others in the same occupation. "It is just like Moscow, only prettier," Alex said to Kostia.

"You'll see," Kostia said. "The world is all the same. What makes you think it will be different in another place? Leningrad is like Moscow, only smaller and handsomer. The south is like the north, only warmer. It is still the world. This is the way it is. I have been a lot of places."

"No," Alex said. "I don't think so. You will be the one to see. It is because of the revolution, here, and the civil war, and the big war, and the famines, and the Czar and the Bolsheviks. That is why it is bad here."

"But don't all countries have all these things, too?"

"No." Alex was always surprised at what these children, who had never been to school, did not know. "It is only Russia that has had all of these things. There is nothing left for the children—no people to care for them, no food for them to eat, no places for them to stay. There are too many of us for the government to care for."

"I should not let the government take care of me, anyway," Kostia said. "Well, we shall see who is right."

There was a government bread store open that day, and Leon and Ivan had found the means to get some loaves. By midafternoon, they were all back at the embankment awaiting Basil. Alex could hardly control his impatience. Would Basil find someone to take them all? It seemed too big a task, now that he thought of it. Would they have to remain here, after their hopes had been raised?

As the time passed when Basil should have appeared,

Alex's anxiety deepened. What had he led his friends to? More misery in the north instead of whatever relief the south might have offered? Alex could feel the minutes of the afternoon tick as if an enormous timepiece hung over his head. The boys grew restless.

"Your teacher's brother is no better than the government," Leon said. "What did you expect? He works for them, doesn't he?"

Alex did not reply.

And then suddenly Basil was there in a rush. "I'm sorry," he said. "They are taking prisoners down the quay and there seemed to be too many police. I thought it better to wait." Then he said, "Boys, can I trust you all? You must understand that I am in danger if you are caught . . . if one of you tells of my involvement." He let this sink in. "Perhaps this would not be so tragic if it were only I. I am only one library worker. But there are many others, like you, who want to leave. Many. If I am not here, fewer can go. We are all part of a lifeline."

Peter said, "We have already talked of that to be sure all here want to go."

"And do you?"

"Ask them," Peter said.

"Who of you want to go?" Basil asked.

Half a dozen arms shot up. Then, one by one, three more, and two more. Then Leon said, "Ah, I don't want to leave the band," and raised his hand, too.

Alex clapped him on the back, but Basil regarded him sharply. "You are sure?" he challenged. "You cannot be a bad link."

"No," Leon mumbled. "I won't be."

"All right," Basil said. "All right." Then he seemed to

withdraw like a turtle inside his overcoat and inside his head, thinking deeply behind a frown. "You see," he said after a bit, "if it were just one of you, it would not be so difficult. Not a lark!" He laughed, and Alex thought it was the first time he had seen this man laugh. "But simple compared with trying to take all of you out. No, that's not so easy."

"But you know we must all go," Alex said anxiously. "Everyone."

"Yes, I understand that," Basil said. "Now, here's what you must do. Tomorrow is Saturday. There are few passenger trains moving then. That is the day the trains of wood come down from the Baltic. You must go down to the station early and wait for the first northbound train and try to get aboard."

Peter laughed now. "No worry," he said. "We can get aboard."

"To tell the truth," Basil said, "you have a better chance your way than traveling second class. You'll stay on until the last stop. You must be careful. That is right across the gulf from Finland and the GPU is looking for people leaving. Also there are many soldiers traveling to Orangienbaum for the holidays."

"We'll be careful," Peter said. "And when we get to the last stop, what then?"

Basil told them what they were to do. Then he took from his pocket a stub of pencil and a piece of crumpled paper. He looked about and counted the children, then wrote "12" and his initial "B" in an elaborate and beautiful script. Then he made a design that looked a bit like the onion dome of a church and in it a tiny cross, but it was so rough one could not really say that was what it was.

"Keep this carefully," he said to Alex, "and give it to the fisherman named Nicholai whom you will find at the end of your journey. You will know him by his red and black beard. He is a fine man. He was in the seminary with me." Then he touched each child on the shoulder. "God be with you," he said.

Night fell on the Touchkoff Quay. The last of the trams rattled by. The gulls nested. And the children finally slept on the precipice of the unknown.

~13

Once again they were in a station, once again the wait, the crowds, and finally the trains of wood. When, eventually, the passenger train arrived, it was already packed with the soldiers traveling to Orangienbaum. Some of the paying passengers on the platform managed to force themselves aboard, hanging onto the steps and pushing through masses of people. Others, less forceful, were left on the platform. Most of the children leapt for their usual places under the cars, although Peter and Alex chose to climb upon the roof for the fresh air.

The train stopped several times, but, approaching their destination, the boys stayed close to the carriages, not risking the train leaving without them. Used to traveling for days, a few hours were a mere moment in time, a flick of the eye. They arrived at the last stop before they knew it. Everyone was getting off the train. The children stayed quietly in their boxes or flattened on the top of the cars until all the soldiers had ambled off in the direction of the rest houses. Then, following Basil's directions, they slipped across the tracks and behind the station. As he had told them, there were two paths leading out into the countryside, one south and one veering off slightly to the northwest, where the sun was low. Anya, well-rested from a long night's sleep and more sleep in her traveling box, kept up with the rest except to complain of what she said were curtains in her eyes. Finally Alex stopped and removed soot from her enormously long eyelashes, and she was off again, scooting among them like a pet dog.

"Slow down," Peter told her. "We are supposed to keep out of sight."

They formed a single line, Peter walking ahead and signaling them to stop whenever he saw anyone or anything in the distance—a cart, a *muzik*. But, in the main, they were walking in open country, rolling slightly up and down, silent and empty. Alex began to wonder if this was, after all, the right road. Basil had said five miles, more or less, but they seemed to have been walking that far, and as yet there were no habitations at all. But off in the distance one could see the gulls, and the wind seemed to gust from there. Perhaps the Gulf of Finland did lie beyond. Alex tried to contain his fears and his impatience.

Now, along a road that paralleled the field, they heard the sound of voices and of tramping feet. Then they saw a horse-drawn wagon with six soldiers such as those they had seen on the train, talking and laughing, passing around a bottle.

"Down!" Peter whispered, and they all flattened out in the field among the dried grasses that poked through the layer of snow, while the soldiers slowly passed and disappeared into the distance. "Now be quiet," Peter ordered. "There may be more."

Anya was tiring, and Alex carried her on his shoulders. She was taller than all of them that way, and before long, she said, "There are some houses just over there. Can you see them?"

136

In a minute they did see them—tiny cottages. The children drew down among the bushes and surveyed them.

"That must be the place," Peter said. "There are three cottages together, just as Basil said."

Once again, Alex was appointed to make the contact. "Remember," Leon said, "it's the first cottage."

They all watched as Alex crossed the road and approached the thatch-roofed buildings. He was observed. A man came out of the first little house. Tall and burly, dressed in heavy fisherman's clothing, he leaned in the doorway. Alex, very frightened, hesitated. He was looking for the special thing that would identify the man as Nicholai, but he was not close enough. Now, yes, he thought he saw it, and, then again, no.

"What is it, comrade?" the man asked. It was too late to turn back. Alex came closer, and, as he did, the man turned fully toward him. In the dimming afternoon light, his beard could be seen, half red, half black.

"I'm Alex," he said. "Are you Nicholai?"

"Perhaps," the man said. "Perhaps not. Why should you ask? And why should I answer you?"

"Because if you are Nicholai, I have a letter from Leningrad for you."

The man looked nervously to the right and left. Down the hill, the gulf glistened under the cold sky. The light was going fast now. "Come in," he said. Alex followed him quickly into the little house, and the man closed the door, then the shutters. He lit a smoky oil lamp, then read the note. "I'm Nicholai," he said. "Where are the others?"

"Across the road and behind the bushes," Alex answered, looking around at the warmth and shelter of this simple cot-

137

tage and feeling a longing to lie beside its hearth and sleep for days.

"Fetch them, but only a few at a time. I will signal when the coast is clear. This is the road to the resort where the soldiers like to stay, and we must be careful. Sometimes they stroll about."

At the signal, Alex sped across the road and fell into the bushes. "It's all right! It's all right!" he whispered, but he felt as if he were shouting. Now a rumbling in the distance announced an approaching cart. It seemed to take forever to come around the curve in the road, and, when it did, it proved to be another cart of soldiers. Nicholai, standing in the doorway, waved to them.

"Have a good vacation, comrades," he called with a smile. But when they passed, his face turned serious as if he had turned off a light. He watched them pass, scowling, then signaled. Alex pushed Kostia, Anya, and Leon on their way. They hurried across the road and into the house. Then the rest, two or three at a time, until he and Peter joined them.

Nicholai surveyed this motley group, huddled in the little room. "First Basil sends me one, then two, then three—'Just this once, Nicholai'—then four. Now look! How many? Twelve? Well, there are twelve months, twelve disciples, why not twelve waifs!" He went to the fire, where water was heating, and made coffee of ground oats. They took turns drinking the scalding liquid from tin cups that were on the hearth. Into a pot at the back of the fire, Nicholai put some potatoes to boil.

Alex felt stunned by all that had occurred. After all these months, here was a grown man taking charge of his comfort and safety, offering food and shelter. Anya was asleep with her head on his lap. He was surprised to find that the tears on her face were his.

Nicholai spoke little at first, except to warn them to be very quiet. After he had given them each a boiled potato, he said, "I am known, in these parts, to be a solitary, bad-tempered fisherman. There are few people living here, but those that are know enough not to bother me. Still, I am thought to live alone here. You must not put yourselves, or me, and any other travelers like yourselves, in danger by making noise, by giving away this place. Should anyone approach, you must all go down here," and he lifted a hatch in the floor. "And quickly."

They were tired, and, despite their excitement, it did not take more than a word from Nicholai for them to curl in a hodgepodge on the floor and sink into slumber. He himself stayed propped in a corner, eyes open, through the night.

Sometime near dawn a loud thud awakened everyone. Then further thumps of something heavy being dragged. The children started for the hatch, but Nicholai signaled them to be quiet and stay where they were. They huddled wide-eyed and frightened as a door slammed. Then Nicholai said, "They are smugglers of alcohol. They use the next cottage as a way-stop. They will be gone at nightfall, but we will have to keep very silent all day. Hush, now."

The day was spent dozing and resting quietly in the little cottage. Nicholai went out a few times so that his life would appear normal. Before he left, he herded the children into the tiny dirt cellar, airless and chill. But when he came back, he brought a string of fish, which he cooked on the fire and gave to the children with tea. As he had predicted, when night fell the thumps were heard again, and the sound of a wagon pulling up to the house. Then the clopping of the horse and the rattling of the wagon announced the smugglers' departure.

"Good!" Nicholai said. "I will tell you the truth; when they arrived I thought they couldn't have picked a worse time. They are always a nuisance. But I had been thinking all night how I could take you all, and their arrival may prove to be the answer to our problem. You see," he said, "my boat is too small for all of you, but the smugglers' boat is large with high sides to shield the cargo."

He filled a jug with fresh water, put some bread in a canvas sack, and said, "Come now. We will make a try for it."

Into the dark they followed Nicholai down to the sandy bank where, at the edge of the water, the ice sparkled blackly and whitely in the moonlight, crunching ominously, almost hungrily, floe against floe. They hid in the bushes while Nicholai surveyed the situation. A small fishing boat was pulled upon the shore and near it a large ketch such as those used for deep-sea fishing. Nicholai threw the jug and sack into this one and was just raising his hand to signal when another fishing boat appeared a few meters down the bank. A man was pushing it over the ice floes, puffing so heavily he could be heard by all. It seemed to take him forever to anchor his boat and take his catch on his shoulder up the bank and out of sight.

When they thought all was clear, two soldiers appeared strolling down the shore, slapping their shoulders to keep warm. When they saw Nicholai, they stopped to talk.

"Out late fishing, comrade?" one soldier asked. Alex's heart skipped.

"No," Nicholai answered, appearing to be working on a rope knot. "Just securing my boat. Last night it shifted with the ice."

"It's beginning to break up," one soldier said. "One of our group tried to walk on it last night when he had a few vodkas in him. We are still thawing him out." They laughed uproariously.

Cold as he had been these last months, Alex could not see the joke in their freezing comrade.

Would they ever go! "We're supposed to be on vacation," one soldier said, "but we get special commendation if we catch anybody escaping. The stationmaster thought he saw some people running across the track. Sometimes we can pull them in like fish, but in this weather not many try it."

"I can understand that," Nicholai said. "It is difficult to get through a sea that is part ice."

And finally, the soldiers tired of the talk or got too cold to stand around. They turned and started back down the shore. "All the same," one called, "keep your eyes open. You can come down to the rest house and tell us. We would see that the local soviet knows of your diligence."

"Thank you, comrades," Nicholai said.

In the bushes, the children were stiff with cold and suspense. Nicholai ordered them to run up and down the shore a bit before he started to organize them for their departure. "We will have to push the boats on the ice a short way, but you must be careful. Push too far and you will be in the water. I will go first, pushing the big boat with Peter and Kostia. Alex, you will push the little boat with Leon." He picked up Anya and put her in the little boat. "The rest of you will follow behind carefully. Don't crowd each other."

With no light but the stars, Nicholai and Peter pushed the smugglers' big boat over the hard ice floes to a point where the ice began to crackle under foot. Then they stopped. Nicholai came back and helped push the boat and lead the others. He nudged the smaller boat until it gently broke through the ice and into the water. Anya was alarmed. "Take me out!" she cried. "I don't want to go to sea."

"Hush!" Nicholai commanded, clapping his hand over her mouth. "Do you want to tell the world you are out here? You're all right. Here are some companions for you," and he lifted two of the smaller children into the boat. Then he held onto the rope and tied it to the larger boat. "The rest of you pay attention, now," he said, and started loading them into the larger boat. "Very carefully, now," he said. "The lightest boy in first, then the next, and so forth. Everyone else be ready to catch onto the sides when it starts to break through the ice." The growling of the ice started when three of them were aboard, and the rest leapt for the gunwales before they got more than their feet wet. Wet feet were nothing new to them.

Now he hauled in the rope and reached into the little boat, transferring the three small children into the larger boat and covering them with sacks. He assigned Alex and Peter to one set of oars and took another pair himself. "We are heading that way." He pointed. "We will use the stars as a guide. We are going north and east. For now, keep the lights from the soldiers' rest house in view. Row straight out from there."

Although neither Peter nor Alex had ever held an oar, they soon caught the rhythm. "Look alive, there," Nicholai called. "You have to pull your weight or we will be all night crossing." Warmed and strengthened by the hot food they had been given while staying in the cottage, and rested from the day of enforced quiet, Peter and Alex were well up to the job of oarsmen, though the water was rough. They pulled together, and the boat fought the wind and the water, breaking through the choppy waves. After the novelty of the sea had palled, the youngest children fell asleep, and the only sound on the water was the creak of the oars, the slap of the waves against the sides of the boats.

Alex's mind was teeming with so many thoughts he found it hard to focus on one. Leaving Russia! How shocked he had been by the idea when Katriana had first mentioned it! Katriana. Basil had said she had really left Russia. Finland! What would they find there? Would he ever see his family again?

"What will it be like, do you think, Peter?" he asked aloud, just to talk, knowing full well that Peter knew no more than he. Less, perhaps.

Peter only shrugged and grunted. Alex had noticed how Peter had grown quiet since Miska's death and the terrible thing at the children's home. Occasionally there were signs of the old Peter, their leader, in charge, but mostly he seemed to be deep inside of himself.

Then suddenly out of the dark night a bright light appeared and approached them quickly. "Hush," Nicholai warned them. "Peter and Alex, get under the sacks with the others! No one say a word."

The light grew closer and proved to be a lantern on the prow of a midsized launch, manned by soldiers.

"Stop and be searched," a soldier called.

"Ahoy, comrade," Nicholai called, through his cupped hands. "I'm glad to see you. Can you point me shoreward? I've lost my bearings."

"Yes? How does a fisherman come to lose his bearings? And how do you come to be fishing so late?"

"I fell asleep and drifted, comrades," Nicholai said, acting sheepish.

"Well, we shall have a look at your boat anyway," the soldier said. "You say you are a fisherman, but there is a lot of smuggling going on here now, and in just such a boat."

Nicholai laughed. "Smuggler! Me! I'm strong," he said, "but do I look strong enough to row a boat full of spirits across the gulf by myself? I wouldn't be home until Friday." And he laughed again.

Under the sacks the children shivered with fear, and Alex held Anya's arms to keep her from squirming. The soldier was just starting to let himself over the side of the launch, preparing to leap into Nicholai's boat, when a call from the deck above stopped him.

"Let's not waste time," an officer told him. "It would take four men to row that boat full of spirits, two at the very least." Then he called, "The shore is that way. Best stay awake, comrade, or you may join the fishes."

They resumed their rowing as soon as the boat was well out of sight, but they were nervous and alert. When they had been rowing for a couple of hours and all arms were aching, Nicholai called a rest. They shipped their oars and the dripping cold water fell upon the faces of some of the sleeping children. They awoke, saying, "Are we there?" Nicholai gave them each a sip of water and a crust of bread.

"What will happen to us when we get to Finland, Nicholai?" Ivan asked.

"There are some people, in a little town near Bjorko, who will see that you have shelter and food until it is decided

144

what it would be best for you to do. Some families may be found in Finland or may have passed through there. Some of you may want to stay. Some may later want to travel farther . . . to Poland, to Germany, to England . . . even to America."

"Why don't you go, Nicholai?" Alex asked.

"Sometime, perhaps, but for now I am a fisherman, and there is still a lot of fishing to be done."

"How will you take both boats back?" Peter now asked, after one of his long silences that Alex had noted. "Isn't this too big to row yourself?"

"I will take just the small one," Nicholai said, "because I must be back by dawn for everything to seem normal. If the smugglers' boat is gone and I am, too, they may make a connection. It would take me too long to row the big one back myself, though I certainly wish I had the use of it again. There is good cover for it a mile or so below my hut where I could hide it. As for the smugglers, I fear they will have to find another boat, anyway."

Alex thought: He has been a student priest in the seminary, but now he is thinking like a thief . . . like us.

Once again, with weary arms, they moved the oars through the water. "It's not much farther," Nicholai said encouragingly. "Keep going."

Only a little later he said, "Now, turn around. See the light on that point? That is Bjorko, Finland. The shore just this side of it is where you are going. Here." He reached into his fishing basket and took out a tallow flare and matches. "After you get a little closer," he said, "you will light this with these matches. Hold it high. When you see a flare in response, make for that point. Some people who watch every night will be there—though they will be surprised to see so many of you." After a few more minutes of rowing, he shipped his oars and stood in the boat.

"Good-bye now, my friends. I will have a hard row to be back by daylight, so I will get a head start. You can do the rest easily. Here." He handed his oars to Kostia and Ivan. "Give it a try, you two." They moved into his seat. "You know what to do," he said, looking at Peter and Alex. "God go with you." And he stepped from the bigger boat into his little fishing craft, untied the rope, and, waving a swift good-bye, turned his little boat and started back the way he had come.

The children were surprised by this sudden move. "But wait," Alex called. "Wait. We have to . . . to thank you. We have to . . . we need . . ."

"Row straight and you will thank me," Nicholai called.

The light on the point seemed much nearer. Pieces of ice now started to crack against the boat. The oars moved small floes through the water. Suddenly, the long-silent Peter was Peter again. "Okay. Now we light the flare," he directed. He reached for the matches. The first went out in the wind. So did the second.

"Be careful," Kostia said. "If we run out of matches, we will not be able to signal."

Peter dove down into the bottom of the boat, sheltering the match and the flare with his body. The last match lit it. The flare was met by applause from all the children, awake and alert now. They raised their heads above the sides of the dory and pinned their gazes on the shore, as Peter held the flare high. They stared hard into the darkness for an answering light.

"How long can it burn?" Leon asked.

"I don't know," Peter said. The torch flickered in the wind.

"Will we live in the boat?" the matter-of-fact Anya asked.

"No," Alex laughed. "We have lived in a cellar, a cave, a train, but we will not live in this boat."

And then, at last, there was a flare of light on the shore just where Nicholai had said it would be. It moved from left to right. Someone was signaling. Peter moved the flare the same way, from left to right. "Come on now," he said. "Let's get back on these oars."

It was harder now without Nicholai's strong arms, even though Kostia and Ivan worked strenuously on their oars. The ice floes were gathering, and the going was slow. Still, the floes seemed less dense than they had been at the start of the journey, and they were able to row nearly to the shore when the boat wedged itself against the ice and would go no farther.

"Out," Peter said. "One at a time. Hold hands and start walking toward the light. Go!" He stood and put Anya on the ice. The others followed, Leon leading, until they were strung out in a line, moving toward the shore where the ice became stronger and stronger.

Kostia and Ivan got out, then Alex. "Come on, Peter," Alex said, steadying the boat for him.

"No," Peter said slowly. "I'm not going."

"Not going!" Alex cried. "What are you going to do, stay here on the ice? Live in the boat?"

"I'm going to go back and . . . and fish with Nicholai."

"You don't know anything about fishing."

Peter laughed, and his laugh rang on the cold ice and water and somehow sounded warm and good to Alex because it sounded like Peter. "I know about *this* kind of fishing. I'm going back to Moscow and get some more children and bring them to Nicholai. I think I shall become a ferryman." He seemed happy for the first time since the terrible events in the south. "Cheer up," he said.

"But Peter, will you ever come back to the band?" Kostia asked.

"Perhaps," Peter said. "When we've fished the sea for all the good fish."

Again, Alex felt the constriction in his throat, the pain of separation that he had come to recognize as the most agonizing pain of all, a pain that cut deeply and then remained to ache.

"No, Peter," he entreated. "Come with us. We are a . . . a family." *Life was stopping again.*

"Yes," Peter said. "And I am going back for others in the family. *Dasvedanya,*" he said. "Say it to all of them for me." And with a mighty pull of the oars, he launched himself back into the gulf, disappearing quickly into a rising mist.

Was the mist on the water or in their eyes? Alex and the others now carefully picked their way across the ice toward the firmer tundra, turning now and then to try and see Peter in the distance, not feeling cold, nor hunger, because the other pain was so strong.

Now they could see the children gathered on the shore, and others—perhaps three or four adults. Their voices carried on the ice. Alex heard someone speaking in accented Russian.

"What a catch! How many fish did we get tonight? Follow me, fish."

He saw someone bend and wrap a blanket about Anya. Then he heard a woman's voice, speaking in perfect Russian. "Thor, please carry this little girl."

148

And Anya, protesting in her toughest voice, "I can walk like the rest."

There was something about the woman's voice that made Alex's heart nearly jump from his chest. And then she turned, saw him, and held out her arms.

Once again, life began.

~ Glossary

BABUSHKA—scarf, or grandmother

BEZPRIZORNI—the wild children. Literally, shelterless

CHORT TZDBYA BEEREE—the devil with you

DASVEDANYA—farewell

DRYAN—selfish bastard

GPU—the secret police

KABUR—thieving by digging tunnels from one building to another

KOMSOMOL—Soviet youth organization

KULAK—landed peasant

KREMLIN—former palace of the Grand Dukes and Czars, now the center of the Soviet government

MATUSA RUS—Mother Russia

MUZIK—peasant

NIEGADZAI—good for nothing

PERYZRONOK—one ring of railroad bell, signaling five minutes to departure

SOOKSIN—son of a bitch

SVOLOTCH—swine

TRETYZVONOK—three rings of railroad bell to indicate that the train is about to leave

ENJOY THESE OTHER GREAT STORIES FROM PUFFIN:

☐ **THE ROOT CELLAR**
Janet Lunn

Rose, a sad and lonely orphan, flees to her aunt's root cellar and emerges to find herself in another century, the world of the 1860s and the chaos of the Civil War where she must save the life of a boy she has come to love.

240 pages   ISBN: 0-14-031835-6   **$3.99**

☐ **MASTER CORNHILL**
Eloise Jarvis McGraw

Michael Cornhill and his foster family lead a happy life in London, until the "Black Death" destroys the city. Sent away when the plague strikes, Michael returns eight months later to find he must try to make a new life for himself.

218 pages   ISBN: 0-14-032255-8   **$4.95**

☐ **THE DOUBLE LIFE OF POCAHONTAS**
Jean Fritz

Caught between two worlds, the Indian princess Pocahontas has to make a painful choice in order to make peace between Captain John Smith's Virginia colonists and her father's tribe.

96 pages   ISBN: 0-14-032257-4   **$3.99**

You can find all these books at your local bookstore. or use this handy coupon for ordering:

Penguin Books By Mail
Dept. BA Box 999
Bergenfield. NJ 07621-0999

Please send me the above title(s). I am enclosing _____
(please add sales tax if appropriate and $1.50 to cover postage and handling). Send check or money order—no CODs. Please allow four weeks for shipping. We cannot ship to post office boxes or addresses outside the USA. *Prices subject to change without notice.*

Ms./Mrs./Mr. _____

Address _____

City/State _____ Zip _____

Sales tax: CA: 6.5%   NY: 8.25%   PA: 6%   TN: 5.5%